ANTHONY RYAN

*This special signed edition is limited to
1000 numbered copies and 26 lettered copies.*

This is copy __860__ .

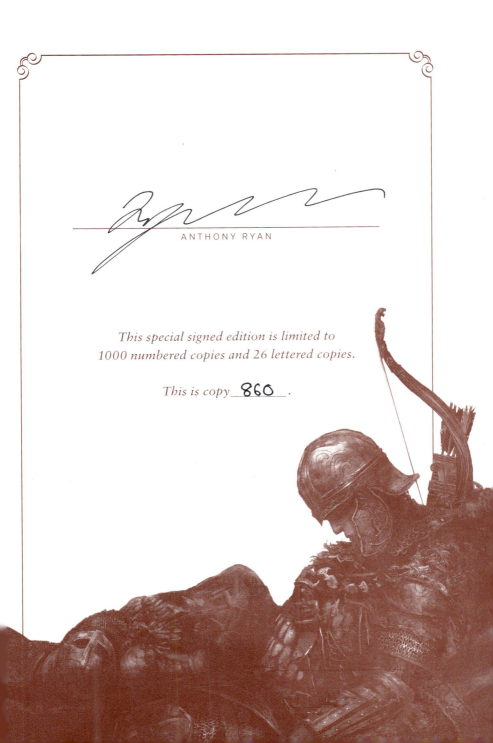

THE ROAD OF STORMS

THE ROAD OF STORMS

THE SEVEN SWORDS
Book Six

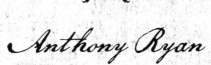

Anthony Ryan

Subterranean Press • 2024

The Road of Storms Copyright © 2024
by Anthony Ryan.
All rights reserved.

Dust jacket illustration Copyright © 2024
by Didier Graffet.
All rights reserved.

Interior illustration Copyright © 2024
by Anthony Ryan.
All rights reserved.

Interior design Copyright © 2024
by Desert Isle Design, LLC.
All rights reserved.

First Edition

Lettered Edition ISBN
978-1-64524-240-6

Limited Edition ISBN
978-1-64524-204-8

Subterranean Press
PO Box 190106
Burton, MI 48519

subterraneanpress.com

Manufactured in the United States of America

To those masters of the battle scene: R. Scott Bakker, George R.R. Martin, Bernard Cornwell, and Akira Kurosawa.

To those who seek glory in life, look not to war
For its blandishments are the darkest of lies.
— *Injunctions of the First Risen.*

Chapter One

THE NAVIGATOR'S PROMISE

•)———(•)———(•

Throughout the unnatural span of his years, Guyime had heard myriad tales of winged, fire-breathing serpents, but Tempest remained the only living specimen he had actually laid eyes upon. Of course, the creature was not a true born example of his mythical kind, but rather a wooden ship's figurehead brought to life by demonic sorcery. In light of this, Guyime was forced to conclude that, if the drakes of legend had ever been real, he would have encountered one before now.

The rainbow sheen of Tempest's emerald scales glimmered in the noonday sun as he responded to his creator's instruction, uncoiling his long body across the *Wandering Serpent*'s foredeck, the perennial twin wisps of smoke trailing from his nostrils. They were darker than usual, Guyime having noticed before that the hue of these effusions reflected the creature's mood. Furthermore, his golden eyes were narrowed in suspicion as he regarded Orsena, a stark contrast to his more typical adoring gaze.

"Don't worry, my dearest," Orsena said, smoothing a hand over Tempest's snout. "It won't hurt. Settle down now, and lie still."

The smoke leaking from the serpent's nostrils thinned to a pale grey, though the narrowness of his eyes persisted. Once he had lowered his elongated bulk to the deck, Orsena gestured at Guyime and the others to place the two wooden contrivances they had constructed on either side of Tempest's body.

"Are you sure this is going to work?" Guyime asked Orsena as they dragged the object to a point halfway along the creature's spine.

"*She* is," Orsena replied, touching a hand to the hilt of the Conjurer's Blade. "Besides, you said we couldn't bring him with us when we make port. As I am unwilling to leave him behind, this is the only alternative acceptable to me."

Guyime concealed a grin and held his tongue. When Orsena adopted the strident, uncompromising tones of the Ultria of House Carvaro, assailing her with questions was not a sound idea.

"Now then," she went on, drawing the demon-cursed blade from her belt, "if you would all be so kind as to step back."

Guyime and Lorweth duly retreated from the nailed-together assemblage of variously shaped and sized timbers. Opposite them, Anselm and Lexius set down their own burden and followed suit.

"She warns this might be a bit brighter than usual," Orsena cautioned, moving to crouch at Tempest's side with the Conjurer's Blade held ready. "So, you would be well advised to shield your eyes."

Lexius, always wary of such things thanks to the magnifying effects of the lenses he wore, swiftly followed her advice.

Anselm and Lorweth also turned their heads, but Guyime chose not to, keen to witness the craft wrought by Orsena. He had seen magic aplenty over the course of several centuries and not yet been blinded by it. The first flare of blue-tinged light from the Conjurer's Blade, however, made him regret his lack of caution.

Pride was ever your worst vice, my liege, Lakorath observed, the smirk evident in his tone as Guyime's eyes snapped closed against the flash. The glow of unleashed magic was accompanied by a deep, resonant thrum that sent a tremble through the deck and put an ache in his ear. It faded with merciful alacrity, Guyime hearing a soft grunt of satisfaction from Orsena and a growl of surprise from Tempest.

"Not yet," Orsena chided when Guyime began to look. "I haven't done the other one."

Another glare tingeing his eyelids red and the same ear-paining thrum and it was done. Blinking tears, Guyime opened his eyes to receive a fierce gust of wind directly in the face. Wiping away the moisture, he beheld a true marvel. It took a lot to impress a soul so riven with wonders, both awesome and awful, but the sight of a serpent rearing to beat newly acquired wings succeeded in drawing a rare laugh from Guyime's lips.

"I'd call that a successful bit of experimenting, my lady," Lorweth said, eyes wide as he took in the remade serpent. "I'll admit to some skepticism, given those wooden abominations we crafted. But who'd have thought they could turn into this?" Guyime saw his point. To his eye, the crudity of the sawed and hacked concordance of planking and off-cuts had borne only a vague resemblance to wings. Now melded into Tempest's flesh, they flared into a display of glittering scales and shimmering membranes that wafted repeated gales across the foredeck. For his part, Tempest appeared enraptured by his remade form, a triumphant gout of fire erupting from his mouth as he swept his wings with ever-increasing energy.

Guyime saw a glimmer of prideful satisfaction in Orsena's bearing as she twirled the Conjurer's Blade. "She says raw materials matter little. It's the intent of the artist that counts."

Beneath her pleased expression, Guyime detected a previously unseen tension in her brow and the set of her jaw.

"What is it?" he asked her, receiving a strained smile in response.

"It didn't hurt before. The Artisan warned it might this time, since the task was so much more intricate. It's the way with her form of magic apparently: complex art requires more energy. But I worried not. Pain is such a rare thing for me, you see."

"Never was there the smallest spark of magic that didn't extract a price, my lady," Lorweth said. "Even from you, it seems. A tot or two of the captain's rum'll set you right. Take it from a druid who's weaved more spells than anyone should…"

His words were interrupted by the strongest gust yet from Tempest. The serpent let out another belch of flame followed by one of his bird-like shrieks as his wings continued to beat, catching enough air to raise his clawed feet from the deck.

"That's enough for now, my dearest…" Orsena began, stepping forward only to reel back as Tempest briefly returned to the deck, crouched, then launched himself upwards. A few sweeps of his wings sent him soaring away across the choppy waves of the Fourth Sea, deaf to Orsena's stern cry commanding that he return at once. He did consent to alter the pitch of his flight and circle the ship, much to the mingled delight and consternation of Captain Shavalla's crew. Then, with a final squawk and a brief spurt of flame, he ascended higher into the air, soon reducing to a vague speck against the blue sky. Within moments, they lost sight of him completely.

"Well, that's a bugger," Lorweth said, breaking the subsequent silence. "Oh well. Mayhap he'll come back when he's hungry." Turning to the stern, he cast a shout at Shavalla. "Some rum, if you please, Captain. For medicinal purposes, you understand."

"And you say this thing can't be trusted." Shavalla peered closely at the Cartographer's chart unfurled upon the map table in her cabin. In recent days, the lines appearing on its surface had taken on a new solidity, displaying a precisely rendered coastline and winding rivers tracing from mountains bordered by a flat plain. The dotted line depicting Ekiri's path described a confused sojourn, circling across the peaks and back again. Although this meandering course conveyed the impression of a lost soul, Guyime harboured severe doubts that was the case.

"It led us into near fatal danger before," he told the privateer captain. "Our quarry is fond of laying traps in our way. Clearly, the Desecrator knows we have a means of tracking his movements."

"Desecrator," Lexius repeated softly, Guyime discerning the telltale cast to his eyes that indicated the inner workings of his remarkable memory. "A name applied to a few historical figures, mainly in the context of religious wars. There are a few older, fragmentary legends that refer to the Infernus, however. Vague allusions to a wrathful demon king, intent on the destruction of all."

Not destruction, Lakorath murmured in Guyime's mind. *If he were to lay waste to this world, he would have no mortals to torment, and that is his ultimate object. Have no doubt of it. The mortal realm will fall if he opens the Infernus Gate, but it will fall into an age of unending cruelty. All the miseries and tortures of the Infernus will be let loose. Humans will be bred purely to suffer. All who live will long for death. Parents will eat their young for the amusement of their demon masters...*

"I understand," Guyime growled, stemming the demon's dire invective. A glance around the cabin at the grim faces of Anselm, Orsena, and Shavalla made it plain that the inhabitants of their swords had conveyed similarly horrifying warnings.

"Before I heard the words of Arkelion's shade at the Spectral Isle," he said, "I imagined that bringing the Seven Swords together might offer the chance of ridding us of their curse. Now we know the truth: they were created to prevent the most dire calamity ever faced by mortal kind. Nor do I believe that we carry these blades due to mere misfortune. The swords were guided to us and we to them by a powerful enchantment woven into the fabric of the world centuries ago. This burden is ours and cannot be shirked. Do any of you gainsay this judgement?"

To his surprise, it was Lexius who broke the subsequent silence. "I cannot fault your reasoning, my lord," the scholar said. "Except to remind you that I carry a blade inhabited by a human soul. Given all we have learned about Arkelion's long-laid plans, I have deduced that my wife was the one fated to bear the Kraken's Tooth. Who better to bear it than so powerful

THE ROAD OF STORMS

a sorceress? In light of Calandra's..." He paused, the apple of his thin neck bobbing as he swallowed. "Calandra's death, I am forced to conclude that Arkelion's scheme cannot be termed infallible, nor its outcome inevitable."

"If you mean we're all highly likely to meet our end before this is over," Shavalla said, "I'd already formed much the same conclusion, scholar. This one is always keen to remind me of that most salient fact." She gestured to the Scarlet Compass sheathed at her belt. Guyime had noted before how she only touched the cursed weapon when she had to. From what the captain had told about her many years of suffering the creature's voice in her head, he had divined that the Navigator was perhaps the most detestable of the four in this curious company.

"Yet she has joined her agency to this enterprise," he said. "Which raises the question whether her guidance can be trusted."

"Trust that she hates the Desecrator more than she hates mortal-kind," Shavalla returned. Her lips bowed in a humourless smile, brows creasing as if in pain. "And a demon's hate is not an easy thing to bear for decades on end, old mate."

Deciding it would be best not to press the matter, Guyime nodded to the map. "Has she any insight to offer on this? Does it show a true track of the Desecrator's steps?"

"Ekiri's steps." Seeker hadn't spoken before now. Having perched herself in the frame of the cabin's window, she had remained in silent regard of the *Wandering Serpent*'s wake. Quietude had been her habit since departing the Spectral Isle with the Morningstar in her possession. It sat in her lap now, cradled as she had cradled Lissah. For her part, the caracal appeared to detest being near the enchanted weapon and now displayed a marked preference for Orsena's company. The fact that Seeker barely seemed to notice the cat's altered mood worried Guyime more than her reticence.

Turning from the window, the beast charmer regarded him with a steady, unblinking gaze. He had looked into the eyes of many a challenger and saw one now.

It's that new toy of hers, my liege, Lakorath advised. *As you've no doubt already guessed. It was made to imbue its owner with both the power to command and the lust to do so, as well as the ability to smash an entire company with just one swipe of that spiked head. I'm impressed by her resistance. Her desire to recover her brat outweighs the seduction of the spell infesting the Morningstar. But rest assured, sooner or later, it will defeat her.* The demon paused in faux contemplation before adding the suggestion Guyime knew he would make: *Kill her now. It'll only be harder later.*

"Quite so," Guyime told Seeker, forcing a smile. "Ekiri's steps. And if we're to find her, we must know where to look without fear of being misled."

"Alcedon," Shavalla stated promptly, inclining her head at the Cartographer's map. "This thing is in agreement with the Navigator, on that point at least. Plus, I recognise the coastline."

"Alcedon," Guyime repeated, peering closer at the chart. "The Realm of the Sun-blessed King."

"You've been there?" Orsena asked, drawing a chuckle from Lorweth.

"I'd wager there's few places his worship hasn't been, your ladyship," the druid said.

"Over a century ago," Guyime said. "A brief mercenary contract that ended badly. I recall a realm mostly at peace, save for raids on its northern border."

"Where lie the Sunless Steppes." Lexius moved to the chart, tracing a finger over the northern mountains and the featureless plain beyond. "Home to the Guhltain horse tribes. Traditional enemies of the Alcedonians. The two have been at war since before the rise of the Valkerin Empire, and long after its fall. If this is to be trusted, Ekiri crossed into the Sunless Steppes some time ago, but has since returned to Alcedon, albeit by a curiously wayward course."

Shavalla stiffened, features betraying a wince of discomfort as a red glow seeped from the edges of her blade's sheath. "She says the Desecrator's intent lies upon the Steppes. But his first attempt to reach it failed. Why, she can't discern, but she senses his rage and the focus of his mind." She pointed to a point on the chart north of the mountains. "Here is where his object lies."

"The Infernus Gate," Guyime murmured. However, the patch of parchment she indicated remained blank of markings. "It must be hidden from the map's sorcery. Concealed beneath the earth, perhaps."

"I think not, my lord," Lexius said. "I believe this to be the site of the ancient city of Nahossa. Alcedon was a vassal state to the Valkerins for three centuries, but prior to that, it had an empire of its own, even laying claim to a portion of the Sunless Steppes. There, a long-extinct Alcedonian dynasty built a city in honour to their gods, a deed that enraged the Guhltain horse tribes who saw it as a desecration of their lands. After years of trying, they succeeded in storming the city and rending it to ruin, though it's said a good deal of impressive architecture remains." He extended a finger to trace a line from the southern mountains. "An Alcedonian emperor once attempted to reclaim Nahossa, leading a great host along the only road ever constructed upon the Steppe. But his army perished en route, supposedly vanquished by whirlwinds conjured via the spell of a Guhltain witch, hence the name this route had borne ever since: The Road of Storms."

"At the end of which lies the Infernus Gate." Guyime straightened from the map, turning to Shavalla. "Which port puts us closest to our goal, Captain?"

She pursed her lips then gestured to a crescent-shaped bay on the Alcedonian coast. "The capital, Creztina. It's a stinking flea pit of a place, as I recall, but I doubt we'll be tarrying there long."

"No, we will not. Your best speed to Creztina then, Captain. I'm sure Master Lorweth will be happy to oblige with a helpful gust or two."

Chapter Two

THE CONSILIO
OF CREZTINA

•———(•)———•

The passage to Creztina obliged the *Wandering Serpent* to navigate channels between a series of islets and the craggy Alcedonian coastline, bringing them within sight of a number of fishing villages and minor ports, or rather, what remained of them.

As ever, our luck holds true, my liege, Lakorath sighed as Guyime surveyed the scorched and tumbled buildings on shore. *It seems we've contrived to arrive in the middle of a war.*

Guyime couldn't fault the demon's judgement. The damage done by a marauding army always bore much the same signature. The grim procession of ruination continued along the coast, indicating the path of a sizeable force making for the capital. However, when they drew close to the port city, the trail of destruction came to an abrupt halt. Guyime had expected to find Creztina under siege, or the plain outside its walls littered with the detritus of recent battle. Instead, it appeared whole and unmolested. As the *Serpent* entered

✣ 21 ✢

the broad arc of the natural harbour to approach the docks, they found it thronged with people. By the time the ship's hull nudged the wharf, the accumulated voices had grown into a cacophony of ribald joy. Guyime looked out upon streets filled with folk lost to revelry and drink. The air was thick with the petals of thrown flowers and the discordancy of many songs sung at full-throated volume.

"If there was a war," Lorweth commented, "it looks like they won."

Guyime would have preferred to await nightfall before disembarking, disliking the prospect of navigating such a multitude. However, time remained their enemy and, given the raucousness of the crowd, he thought it likely this celebration would wear on for days.

"Happy sailing and good fortune, old friend," Shavalla told Cora at the head of the gangplank. "She's yours now."

The well-muscled first mate was not given to overt emotion, but strove to contain tears as she watched her captain run a hand over the *Wandering Serpent's* rail. "We'll wait for you, Captain," she said. "As long as it takes."

"No." Shavalla shook her head, smiling, though her voice was firm. "No waiting, Cora. That's my final order to you. Sail this fine ship and her excellent crew far from here and set yourselves to working the trade routes. I think you've all had your fill of danger."

Guyime knew that, should Shavalla command it, Cora and the entirety of her crew would follow their captain into whatever dangers waited ashore. In fact, he had considered persuading her to do just that, since two dozen seasoned fighters might well come in handy. Yet, he didn't. Shavalla entertained few illusions regarding her likely fate, and would not abide leading her sailors into so dark a future. After sharing a final embrace with Cora, she straightened and descended the gangplank without a backward glance.

"Any notion of where to find horses in this city?" she asked Guyime when they joined the others on the quay. "We'll need a few if we're to traverse the Steppes."

"House Carvaro has substantial interests in this port," Orsena said. Lissah squirmed in her arms, the caracal hissing in annoyance at the proximity of so many ill-smelling humans. "I'm sure my appointed agent will be able to provide horses and provisions." The Ultria frowned, casting her gaze around the jostling throng. "If only I had any notion of where to find them."

Questioning of the less drunk townsfolk produced directions to the Mercantile Offices of House Carvaro, whilst also providing an explanation for the celebration. "Rebel swine have fled, 'aven't they?" a cheerfully tipsy woman of impressive proportions informed Guyime. Her pendulous, wine-soaked breasts had spilled from the confines of her dress, but she didn't appear to care. "Pished off back to their mountain hovels where they belong," she added, offering a belch for emphasis. "Traitorous cowards."

Fortunately, the agent of House Carvaro proved to be both sober and more informative. Initially, Orsena's pounding on the door to the substantial and ornate marble edifice of the mercantile house had produced a strident response that the establishment was closed for business.

"Would you leave your Ultria standing in the street?" Orsena called back in the perfectly phrased and cultured Atherian of the Exultia caste, whereupon the door was swiftly opened.

Guyime felt House Carvaro's agent to be surprisingly young for her role. Garbed in a grey and black dress completely lacking in ornamentation, she exuded an air of severe efficiency. The impression was enhanced by her tightly bound black hair and angular features untouched by paint save for a dark shade of red pigment upon her lips. Upon being summoned by a panicked underling, she reacted to Orsena's arrival with only a slight raise of her pencil-thin eyebrows before offering a bow of appropriate depth.

"Evehla Toressi, Ultria," she said in smoothly spoken Atherian. "Consilio of House Carvaro's interests in the Realm of Alcedon and the northern environs of the Fourth Sea. I am at your service."

"An Atherian name," Orsena observed.

"Yes, Ultria. I enjoy the privilege of having been born to the Ervitsia caste, although, like you, I have been compelled to forsake my mask. The locals take exception to such things. Long ago, one of their gods supposedly avowed a dislike of facial coverings on the grounds that they signify a deceitful soul."

Guyime knew the Ervitsia to be the order of Atherian society tasked with administering the city's bureaucracy or the affairs of the Exultia, like the unfortunate Investigating Magistrate Tolemio Lucarni. He had been a man of considerable circumspection, not to mention dedication to his allotted role in life. Seeing the mix of expectation and careful respect on the face of Evehla Toressi as she offered a second bow, Guyime judged her to be of a similar disposition.

"It shall, of course," she told Orsena with grave assurance, "be my pleasure to assist you in any way."

"Excellent." Orsena scratched between Lissah's ears when the caracal let out a peevish mewl. "You can start by fetching some meat for this one. The fresher and bloodier the better. After that, I should like a fulsome description of recent events in this kingdom. Oh, and," she flicked a hand at Guyime and the others, "some refreshment for my companions, too, if you wouldn't mind."

"The rebellion began over three years ago, and the reasons for it are varied and hotly debated." Evehla stood at the head of a large table in what she described as the house's Appointments Room. A procession of servants had piled an assortment of food and drink onto the table, though only Lorweth and Lissah chose to partake of the bounty.

"My thanks for this most generous hospitality, m'lady," the druid said, cheek bulging with a morsel of chicken as he raised a goblet in the agent's direction. The evident interest in the gaze he allowed to linger on Evehla's trim form bespoke a hunger for something besides sustenance. The agent responded to his comment with the smallest curve to her lips before returning her full attention to her employer.

"However," she went on, "the spark that lit this revolt was much the same as all others: want. People in the northern hill country suffered a series of poor harvests and harsh winters. Their tribulations were made worse when King Daxos decided to levy yet higher taxes to make up for the revenue lost to wasted crops. Consequently, people began to starve. There were just a few violent incidents at first, crown storehouses raided and tax collectors beaten. This, in turn, prompted the king to send more troops into the region, resulting in a series of massacres amongst the more militant villages. A full-blown uprising started shortly thereafter, led by a man named Rajan Darric. Although reputedly just a simple farmer, he had a strong arm, a knack for inspiring loyalty, and considerable cunning. Within months, all the royal garrisons in the north had been wiped out or driven into retreat. Alcedon had effectively become two nations, and there it might have ended. With the king's treasury empty, he had little hope of mustering an army strong enough to take back to the north. The rebels began acclaiming Rajan a king in his own right and there were whispers from court that Daxos would be forced to agree to a treaty with this peasant upstart. Yet Rajan, it transpired, was not interested in peace.

"Marching his rebel host south, he sacked over a dozen towns and cities in an unbroken string of victories. City walls fell before him. Reports differ as to how this was achieved, although wild stories of Rajan's invincibility flew far and wide. The few who survived encountering Rajan in combat spoke of him wielding a mighty tulwar capable of sundering any armour and shattering any blade."

The agent fell silent when her audience stirred at this, Guyime exchanging glances with the others. "Arkelion made mention of a warlord," Lexius said. "And there are recurrent tales from the distant east of warriors made invulnerable by a darkly enchanted tulwar."

"And so the world tilts to place another sword in our path," Guyime mused before inclining his head at Evehla. "Please continue."

The Road of Storms

"Daxos, of course, couldn't simply allow the rebel horde to advance unopposed. He dispatched his martially inclined daughter, Princess Lyntia, to intercept them with twenty thousand troops. At first, it seemed she would do rather well. Unlike other hosts her father had sent forth, her army was not beset by desertion and discord, maintaining a disciplined march all the way to their dire fate. Yet, when battle came, it proved a calamity of the first order. Rajan feigned a retreat to draw the princess into a valley, whereupon his forces swept down from the hills to assail her flanks. Her ranks broken, Princess Lyntia fled back to Creztina with barely a few hundred Royal Guardsmen. The capital was now naked before the Rebel King. Then, just three days ago, word arrived that the horde had changed direction. Instead of continuing their inexorable advance to seize the heart of Alcedon, they turned north and marched home." Evehla paused to raise her brows a fraction. "It was certainly a relief, as the documentation required to agree to fresh trading terms with a new monarch would have been highly burdensome."

"Do you have any notion as to why the Rebel King chose to turn away?" Orsena asked. "I assume this house maintains a network of keen-eyed informants."

"Indeed we do, Ultria. Sadly, all they have been able to offer is weak rumour and bizarre tales of some bewitching foreigner that I find hard to credit."

The Morningstar's spiked head crunched into the table as Seeker rested a hand upon it, getting to her feet. "Bewitching foreigner?" she repeated, fixing Evehla with a hard, demanding stare. "Describe her."

The agent was plainly a difficult woman to intimidate, yet the beast charmer's glare was sufficiently unnerving for her

❖ 27 ❖

to cast a nervous glance at Orsena. Receiving a nod, she gave a small cough before speaking on. "I haven't set eyes on her myself, of course, but our informants speak of a beauteous and youthful maiden with the appearance of one who hails from the lands south of the Second Sea. Where or how she came into contact with the Rebel King is unknown, as is the true scale of her influence. Perhaps she is simply his lover, despite the many lurid rumours regarding the wicked enchantment she supposedly cast over Rajan's mind. All hard to credit, as I said. What is beyond doubt is that, not long after taking her into his camp, he turned his host north."

"Then that is where we go." The Morningstar left deep scars in the table's polished surface as Seeker dragged it clear. "Instead of tarrying here…"

"She has the bearer of a demon-cursed blade in her thrall," Guyime cut in, halting Seeker's progress to the door. "And therefore, his army, too. Defeating so many is beyond even our powers."

"Your powers, perhaps, Pilgrim," Seeker returned, raising the Morningstar. The links of the weapon's chain began to glow a fiery shade of orange as she grasped them tight. "I have strength of my own now."

"Go after her alone and you'll die," Guyime stated, staring into Seeker's eyes. "And Ekiri will still be a slave to the Desecrator's will."

He held her gaze, watching her rage simmer and the glow of the Morningstar's chain blossom before it began to flicker and fade. Guyime swallowed his relief as she stalked back to the table, the tendons of her neck standing out as she mastered herself.

Still enough of her own will left to contend with the Morningstar's spell, Lakorath judged. *Though, how much longer she'll last...*

"Consilio Evehla," Guyime said, turning back to the agent. "What estimates do you have regarding the strength of the rebel host?"

If talk of demon-cursed blades and a display of ensorcelled weaponry discomfited her in any way, Evehla failed to show it. "At first, the king's officials were at pains to downplay their numbers and their capabilities," she replied promptly. "Describing Rajan's forces as a rag-tag bunch of barely-clothed hill farmers, no more than a few thousand strong at most. Princess Lyntia's defeat put paid to such nonsense. The best estimate from our own reports is a strength of at least thirty thousand. Although they have suffered from the diseases and desertions that afflict all armies on campaign, to date they have displayed a remarkable cohesion and dedication to their cause."

Rather like that mob of yours after we rekindled your own rebellion, my liege. Lakorath gave a wistful sigh. *That curious mingling of love and hate they exuded was certainly a potent brew. They would have followed you to, well, the death, which most did, after all. This Rebel King is a man in your mould. Killing him won't be easy, especially if he's bearing steel inhabited by a warlord drawn from the Infernus. You can bet the stratagem that won him victory over the luckless princess was the demon's notion. To fight such an army, you will need one of your own.*

"We do have intelligence on the Rebel King's likely intentions," Evehla ventured as Guyime's thoughtful silence continued. "If, as seems wise, we discount the tales of his alluring witch, it's fair to assume that, rather than lose so many lives in storming the capital, he simply decided to go home. Having spared Creztina, he is in a position to seek amicable terms with King Daxos. With no royal army to oppose him, he will consolidate his gains in the north, construct fortifications..."

"The Rebel King is not going home, Consilio," Orsena interrupted with an appreciative smile. "But I thank you for your diligence, which will not be forgotten when your annual bonus is calculated. We shall require detailed maps of the northlands and the Sunless Steppes, especially as they pertain to the region around the ruins of Nahossa. Also, please provide a list of any guides familiar with the region, especially those with knowledge of the less well-known routes."

"Stealth won't help us," Guyime said. "Not with this."

"Why not?" she asked. "With proper guidance, if we move swiftly enough, we can get ahead of the Desecrator, beat him to Nahossa and destroy what lies there."

"If I may, Ultria," Evehla said, bowing once again to diminish any sense of insult that might arise from contradicting her employer. "There are certainly covert paths through the mountains, but if Nahossa is your object, there is no alternative but to journey across the Sunless Steppes. Your party would inevitably attract the notice of the Guhltain, who do not tolerate outsiders upon their land."

"As they didn't tolerate the Desecrator when he tried to venture there," Guyime said, thinking back to the wayward course plotted on the Cartographer's Map. "That's why he turned back and sought out the Rebel King. He needs an army to reach the gate. As we'll need one to stop him reaching it."

"But where to find one, my lord?" Lexius asked. "We are strangers here."

"True," Guyime agreed, turning to Orsena with a tight smile, "but one of us happens to be wealthy enough to buy every sword in this benighted kingdom. Consilio Evehla, please be good enough to arrange an audience with King Daxos for myself and Ultria Orsena."

Chapter Three

THE COURT OF THE SUN-BLESSED KING

According to Evehla, arranging a royal audience required three bribes of exorbitant size. They were paid to separate officials occupying successively higher positions in the hierarchy of the Alcedonian court. From her peeved expression, Guyime wondered if she were more annoyed at the expense or the inefficiency of being forced to conduct repeated negotiations. Still, thanks to her exhaustive efforts, Guyime and Orsena found themselves walking through the palace gates only two days after arriving in Creztina.

Casting an appraising glance over the tall spires of the royal palace, Guyime judged it the architecture of opulence rather than practicality. "Built to impress, not withstand an assault," he commented to Orsena. "Home to a dynasty that has known peace for too long."

"You disapprove of peace, your highness?" she enquired. "I would have thought it a laudable achievement for any royal house."

"Peace breeds weakness, my father used to say." Guyime grunted a mostly humourless laugh. "But then, he was also a fool and a braggart."

"Whether built for peace or war, it's certainly seen better days." Orsena nodded to the steps ahead of them, the edges and joins of which were rich in cracks. "My always opinionated companion," she went on, resting her palm on the pommel of the Conjurer's Blade, "has a way of seeing into the fabric of buildings, and judges this one to be only a few years away from total collapse."

"As goes the castle, so goes its lord," Guyime muttered. Another of his father's sayings, one he felt possessed more wisdom than most of the old man's pronouncements.

The myriad roads walked in Guyime's long life had brought him to many a royal palace to stand before many a monarch. Common to all such events was the ritualised tedium required to perform the relatively simple task of entering a room. Being conveyed into the presence of King Daxos was no exception. Upon ascending the steps to the tall, pointed arch of the palace entrance, they were greeted by a coterie of courtiers and escorted to a succession of rooms, each one larger and more ornately decorated than the last. Prolonged intervals of waiting were interrupted by following a yet more finely attired functionary along corridors of varying length until, at last, they were admitted to the throne room of the Sun-Blessed King.

It was a vast, circular chamber of tall columns supporting a domed ceiling emblazoned with a motif of the sun. The great shimmering circle was gilded and surrounded by a host of figures Guyime knew represented the Alcedonian pantheon of gods. In the centre of the sun, an aperture allowed a single ray

THE ROAD OF STORMS

of sunlight to stream down to the chamber floor to illuminate a throne occupied by a man of impressive girth. A twenty-strong contingent of guardsmen were arrayed in a semi-circle behind the throne, and to either side stood a pair of contrasting figures. On the king's right was a young man clad in an ensemble of silken finery with a thin golden band upon his head. To his left stood a woman of approximately the same age, wearing a suit of gold-embossed armour. Guyime took note of the fact that, despite her martial appearance, she wore no weapon. Also, the tiara sitting amidst her dark hair was considerably smaller than the golden band worn by the young man. Thanks to Evehla's fulsome briefing, he knew these to be the king's eldest children: Prince Ihkanos and the recently defeated Princess Lyntia.

"Hated rivals since childhood," the Consilio had advised. "Born to different concubines. Ihkanos is the elder by only two weeks and lacks his sister's interest in all things warlike. However, his greed and facility for intrigue make him a figure not to be underestimated."

As Guyime and Orsena followed prior instructions by both sinking to their knees and lowering their foreheads to the marble tiles, a courtier held forth in a booming voice: "King Daxos, Eighth of His Name, Sun-Blessed King of Alcedon and Overlord of the Ardrus Nuarem, bids you welcome."

Custom dictated that courtly visitors remain in the same servile position until the king gave them leave to rise, something Guyime felt required an excessive amount of time. When the king finally spoke, his voice was a rasping echo bespeaking a considerable weariness. "And who are these who come before us this day?"

❖ 35 ❖

"Ultria Orsena Carvaro, my king," a far less weary voice said, presumably the prince. "And her mercenary captain, so I'm told."

"Carvaro, eh?" The king let out a sigh. "Thought that greedy bugger died months ago."

"He did, my king. This, I believe, is his daughter and heir."

"Oh." Another sigh, then a whisper that Guyime's ears couldn't catch, but Lakorath's demonic senses could. *He's asking how much the crown still owes House Carvaro. The boy says it's quite the sum. And they've defaulted on the last three payments. It appears we find ourselves in the court of a beggar king, my liege.*

"Rise," the king's faltering command echoed across the tiled floor. "Come forth so that we may better hear your words."

Getting to their feet, Guyime and Orsena approached until they reached the band of red tiles a dozen feet from the throne. Evehla had warned against staring at the monarch, but Guyime found his gaze lingering on this plainly afflicted man. He felt it curious that the mix of ailments besetting King Daxos should make him appear simultaneously corpulent and emaciated. His head, rendered small beneath the golden crown he wore, resembled a skin-wrapped skull perched upon a bloated neck, the damp flesh blotched with grey and red marks. The rest of his form was hidden by the shimmering cloak that descended curtain-like to the floor, but even from this remove Guyime could smell the sickly melange of sweat and urine emanating from its folds.

Ugh, Lakorath snorted in disgust. *He's got more drugs in him than a whole street of apothecaries. I doubt he's walked anywhere in years. This king has no more than months left to reign and I get the sense that his son still thinks that too long a wait.*

The Road of Storms

"Most eminent king," Orsena said, bowing low. "Please accept my deepest gratitude for agreeing to receive our unworthy presence."

The king's eyelids narrowed over the bulging orbs set into his skull. "I met your father once," he said. "He wasn't anywhere near so pleasing to look upon. And he only consented to bow but once."

"I shall be happy to bow as many times as you like, sire." Orsena once again lowered her head.

Something that might have been a smile twisted the cracked lines of the king's lips. "Heh. Not here for money, then?"

"Indeed we are not, sire. In fact, I come to forgive all debts owed to House Carvaro by the realm of Alcedon. It is my fervent hope that, by this act, you will afford my words with the trust they deserve. For I come with grave tidings."

This heralded a pause during which Daxos exchanged glances with his son. Guyime saw the prince raise an eyebrow, whereupon the king gave a slight nod.

"Such largesse is, of course, appreciated," Prince Ihkanos said, smiling as he inclined his head at Orsena. "However, I am charged by the king with ascertaining all dangers to this realm." His eyes flicked towards Guyime. "Therefore, I am bound to express concern regarding the presence in this city of one who reputedly had a hand in the destruction of Carthula and the massacre of the Atherian Exultia caste." He paused to broaden his smile. "Yes, we have heard of you. The stories grow more lurid and outlandish by the day. Most recently, I heard a tale regarding a kraken roused from the deep and set to destroy the fabled Spectral Isle of the Fifth Sea."

✣ 37 ✣

"It wasn't a kraken," Guyime said. "And it was already roused." He allowed a deliberately prolonged pause before adding in a flat tone, "My prince."

A small sound came from Princess Lyntia; Guyime saw her lower her head to conceal a grin. Her brother had plainly heard her smothered mirth and was noticeably less amused.

"Kraken or not, I note you do not deny these tales," he said, voice pitching higher and a pinkish hue colouring his cheeks. "The Ultria speaks of grave tidings. Is it not the case that you, in fact, represent the greatest danger? Everywhere you tread, destruction seems to follow. There are some who name you the Doomwalker."

That's a new one, Lakorath chimed in. *Certainly has a ring to it, don't you think?*

"I am a danger only to those who would choose to be my enemy," Guyime returned. He met the prince's gaze squarely, not troubling to voice the expected honorific.

He didn't like that. The demon's observation was redundant, since Ihkanos's rage was evident in his quivering features. *This is so fucking tedious,* Lakorath went on with a groan. *Just kill them all and seize the throne. Then you can raise all the armies you like.*

"Perhaps," Orsena said in a carefully diplomatic tone, "the king would care to hear my tidings before passing judgement prejudiced by ill-informed rumours."

Ihkanos started to speak again, but his words faltered when a skeletal hand emerged from the confines of his father's cloak. "Allow our guest to continue, my son," he said, his voice yet thinner than before. "I've little doubt I shall find her words diverting, and diversion is something to be craved at my age."

THE ROAD OF STORMS

"My thanks, sire." Orsena straightened before speaking on, addressing herself to Daxos alone. "It is my misfortune to inform you that the recent deliverance of this city from destruction at the hands of the rebel horde is but temporary. The traitor Rajan has not turned his army north with the intention of consolidating his hold on prior conquests. House Carvaro has obtained unambiguous intelligence that the so-called Rebel King intends to march to Nahossa, there to seize something that will afford him unimaginable power. With this thing in his grasp, he will pose a threat not just to Alcedon, but all the Five Seas, even the lands beyond. I have set all the resources of my house to preventing this calamity, and come before you now to plead that you join us in this enterprise."

From the confusion on the old king's knitted brows, Guyime doubted that this was the diversion he had craved. Prince Ihkanos appeared yet more confused, lips squirming as he struggled to formulate a response. His sister, however, had no trouble finding her voice.

"Rajan already possesses an ensorcelled weapon," Princess Lyntia stated. Her gaze, steady and narrow in scrutiny, flicked between Guyime and Orsena. A defeated commander she was, but Guyime saw clearly that she was also no fool. "That damn tulwar of his," she added. "Why would he have need of whatever lies in an ancient ruin?"

"Because, Princess," Orsena replied, "that very tulwar has twisted his already disturbed mind into a festering cauldron of unquenchable ambition. The blade he carries is powerful, of that there is no doubt, but it is a mere trifle compared to what lies in Nahossa."

"And what is that?" The princess's eyes narrowed further. "Precisely."

Orsena paused. Those not so attuned as Guyime to the nuances of her perfect features would have missed the small line in her brow, reflecting an abiding discomfort with deceit. Before coming here, she had argued for a bald statement of the honest facts: they were in pursuit of a high-ranking demon intent on opening the Infernus Gate. A laudable mission sure to garner the support of any sane person, if they believed it. However, Guyime's extensive experience of human weakness, in all its varied forms, left him in no doubt that such a tale would invite only incredulity and scorn. So, after a discussion with Lexius, they had concocted what Guyime hoped would be a convincing fiction, one bound up with enough truth and the temptation of reward to arouse both belief and avarice in a king.

"I am sure I need provide no lessons to this court regarding the history of Nahossa," Orsena began. "A mighty complex of temples built in honour of the gods, fallen to the barbarians of the Sunless Steppe. The tale is ancient and oft told. What has become lost over the many centuries since its creation is that Nahossa was more than just impressively shaped stone and brick. Contemporary accounts speak of an offering to the gods that outshone any made before. A thousand bulls were sacrificed in their honour, along with ten thousand slaves. But, sire, your ancestors had more than blood to offer the gods.

"Amongst our company, we count ourselves blessed by the presence of the finest scholar of our age. As Prince Ihkanos is so well informed regarding our travels, he can attest to the veracity of this description. Our scholar has unearthed documents which relate how the entire citizenry of the Alcedonian Empire were required to surrender one quarter of all the gold they possessed to the construction of Nahossa. He has also established, beyond doubt, that when the city stood complete, a substantial portion of that wealth remained unspent and, as the ultimate signal of his devotion, the emperor ordered it concealed beneath the temple to Ixius, the mightiest of gods. There it lies still, undiscovered by the Guhltain barbarians, but now revealed to the one who styles himself the Rebel King."

"Revealed how?" the princess enquired.

"You will no doubt have heard how Rajan has recently taken up with a foreign witch. Some count her merely his lover, but I can assure you she is far more than that. Her youthful appearance is but a facade concealing a much older creature possessed of arcane knowledge, and she is intent upon claiming the treasure of Nahossa for herself. With such vast riches, she could buy whole kingdoms without need of conquest."

"As could House Carvaro," Ihkanos said. Guyime saw plentiful suspicion on the prince's face, but also a familiar gleam in his eye.

He swallowed it all, my liege, Lakorath confirmed. *Bait, hook, and twine. The king too, with some reservations. The princess remains unconvinced, but I sense the hunger of one presented with an opportunity. Her defeat at Rajan's hands has left her ulcerating for vengeance.*

"The Road of Storms is not to be trodden lightly," Ihkanos continued. "Even for those of such dire reputation." His lips curled a little as he cast a sideways glance at Lyntia. "As my sister can attest."

Guyime saw the princess stiffen in response, fists bunching at her sides in a manner that indicated an urge to reach for a weapon. However, she maintained a rigid silence as her brother spoke on.

"For that is your true object, is it not?" he demanded. "Follow the Road of Storms to Nahossa and take this great treasure for yourself?"

"House Carvaro has already incurred considerable expense on this enterprise," Orsena pointed out. "Not to mention willingly surrendering the interest that would otherwise accrue from your family's considerable debt to us. Some measure of fair compensation would seem appropriate."

The prince's already reddened features deepened into a crimson hue as he began to stutter out a reply, once again falling silent at a flap of his father's hand. King Daxos appeared ever more weary as he settled a faint smile upon Orsena, all formality stripped from his voice as he asked, "How much?"

"Given the risks, and the expense…" Orsena paused for contemplation. "Half would seem reasonable."

"You demand half the treasure that is by rights the property of this realm?"

Orsena bowed again, lower than before. "Of course, sire, you are free to claim it yourself, without our assistance."

Ihkanos began to stutter again, but his father paid him no heed, instead turning to Lyntia. "And what say you, my valiant daughter?"

Before replying, the princess subjected Orsena and Guyime to a yet fiercer bout of scrutiny, her eyes lingering on their swords. Her brother was well informed about their prior sojourns, but the weight of her gaze upon the demon-cursed blades made Guyime suspect that her level of knowledge went even deeper.

THE ROAD OF STORMS

"Rajan has several days march on us," she said eventually. "And a great host at his back. At most, this realm can field perhaps two thousand warriors, all cavalry. With careful choice of route, we might beat him to Nahossa, but would have no hope of defeating him when he arrives. That's if we survived the Guhltain's attentions upon the Road of Storms. We stand in severe want of swords to achieve this goal."

"Then, Princess," Orsena told her, "we'll just have to buy some more, won't we?"

Chapter Four

THE STONE DOG

•———(•)———•

Like most major ports, Creztina boasted an extensive dockside slum populated mainly by non-natives. In time of war, it was common for those wishing to sell their swords to congregate in such places. If the pay was reputed to be good, the haul of mercenaries would be substantial, and often rich in fighters of great renown and free companies of veteran warriors. If not, the pool of recruits could be shallow indeed. Judging by the assembly of disparate folk gathered on the dock the following morning, Guyime concluded that many of the more skilled sellswords drawn to this realm during the rebellion had long since departed. Consilio Evehla had been industrious in spreading the word that a new and very well paid contract was on offer. The rumoured terms had been so generous as to swell the crowd to near four thousand, but far from all were fighters. Some were sailors lured away from their ships by the prospect of riches, and many more were townsfolk compelled to seek out the only labour to be had in an impoverished city.

He chose to address them from the deck of one of House Carvaro's larger freighters, setting Lorweth to the task of

※ 45 ❖

speaking first. The druid had a gift for invective and Guyime hoped some suitably inspiring oratory would fire the enthusiasm of their potential recruits.

"Know you not who stands before you?" Lorweth asked the crowd, one hand grasping the port shrouds as he leaned out to cast his voice across the sprawl of upturned faces. "This," the druid flourished a hand at Guyime, "is none other than the Stone Dog himself. Yes, friends! In years to come, you will be able to say that, with your own eyes, you looked upon the greatest captain of hired swords ever to travel the Five Seas. With him at the head of our host, can any doubt our victory? And know that, at the conclusion of this contract, victory over the rebel filth will reap the richest bounty!"

Lorweth raised both voice and arm upon speaking the final word. The expected cheers, however, failed to materialise. Instead, some in the crowd exchanged muttered doubts whilst most remained silent save for a smatter of uncertain coughing.

"Not the easiest audience, your worship," the druid murmured to Guyime as he stepped down from the rail. "Warmed them up as best I could."

Taking his place, Guyime surveyed the faces below, finding wariness on most, and desperation on a few. He couldn't help but reflect on the hosts he had commanded in the past. As the Ravager, he had led tens of thousands from one end of the northlands to the other and counted every soldier, both loyal and skilled with the arms they bore.

Hardly the foundation of an army, my liege, Lakorath observed, echoing Guyime's doubts. *I'd guess two out of three will make for the hills with their first day's pay when we're a mile beyond the city gate.*

THE ROAD OF STORMS

Guyime didn't doubt the demon's judgement and would have spent all of Orsena's fortune to secure the services of just a thousand of his veterans. Not that any still drew breath. *Neither will this lot before long,* Lakorath chuckled, unable to resist a jibe. *But what choice have you, my liege?*

"My friend speaks true when he names me a captain of mercenaries," Guyime said, summoning the booming tones that had once sent thousands into battle. "I have led many to war in many lands, and I tell no lie when I say that I have never failed to complete a contract. If you are to march with me you must know this, so that you understand that I will stomach neither shirker nor coward. Some of you may choose to join us because you have accounts to settle with the rebels. This is well and good, for you will be provided fulsome opportunity for vengeance. Some will join because they wish nothing more than a full belly. This is also well and good, for in truth I care not why you fight, only that you do.

"To make clear the terms of your service, hear this: all who make their mark upon the contract will undertake to follow orders without question and never retreat unless by leave of their captains. Nor will you loot nor visit any harm upon the people of this land. Failure to meet these terms will result in flogging for a first offence and death for a second. I strongly urge you not to test my resolve in this, for I am happy to provide ample demonstration if needed. Upon making your mark, you will receive one silver Atherian talent. After twenty days on the march you will receive another. At the conclusion of this campaign, all who answer the muster will receive five gold talents. These terms apply to all and are not for negotiation, regardless of prior reputation."

Pausing to gauge the effect of his words, Guyime read shrewd calculation in the faces of the experienced fighters, naked avarice amongst the sailors, and only pathetic need in the townsfolk. For most, the pay for this campaign represented riches they could never hope to accrue in a lifetime of toil. He knew Lakorath was right: many would melt away on the march, content with their one silver coin. But others would stay, their desertion delayed by the prospect of a second. By the time they reached the Road of Storms, he would count himself fortunate if half still marched under his word. Five gold talents provided a powerful enticement, but even the most fervent greed could be undone by simple fear.

"Line up there to make your mark, receive your coin, and take your billet." Guyime pointed to the trestle table Evehla had set up on the wharf and the dozens of tents beyond. He counted on the presence of a full company of royal guards under personal command of Princess Lyntia to discourage desertions before they departed the city come the morning.

"We march with the dawn, so be sure to take your leave of any loved ones before making your mark. And," Guyime paused to cast a hard, promissory glower across the crowd, taking time to peer directly into as many faces as he could, "remember my words this day. Shirkers and cowards are not wanted. If I have to hang any of you for forgetting, I'd best not hear any bleating about it."

◆——◆——◆

"It occurs to me, Captain," Princess Lyntia said, "that I have been remiss in not formerly setting out the command arrangements for this host."

The Road of Storms

The princess, Guyime, and Orsena viewed the untidy ranks of newly enlisted soldiers traipsing through the city's northern gate from atop a low hill outside the walls. Guyime sat astride a sturdy grey mare from House Carvaro's stables whilst Lyntia rode a warhorse, a striking beast of finely bred muscle, black from head to tail. Orsena had procured herself an ivory-hued stallion that outshone the princess's steed, both in beauty and stature. Guyime had noticed an uncharacteristic disdain upon the Ultria's face when in Lyntia's presence and suspected her choice of mount to be far from accidental. He was unsure what it was about the princess that irked Orsena so. His brief acquaintance with Lyntia revealed her to possess a cutting tongue and harshness in the manner with which she delivered orders to her guards. However, he had yet to see any signs of true malice.

She senses her ravening need for retribution, Lakorath explained. *Or rather, that pretentious bitch in the Conjurer's Blade does. The perfect daughter of House Carvaro was created to be above such things. She doesn't understand it, so, as is the way with mortals, tends to detest it in others.* The demon paused to laugh. *One day, she's going to fully comprehend the fact that she isn't actually human. When that happens, I do wonder what she'll become.*

"Command arrangements, highness?" Guyime said.

"Yes." Lyntia afforded him a patently empty smile. "I apologise for not addressing the matter sooner, but everything has been so hectic these past two days." She extended a hand to the host trooping through the gate. "Whilst many of our recruits are foreign mercenaries, many more are subjects of this realm. Therefore, it is only fitting that overall command of this host resides with me."

"Subjects or not," Orsena said, "all of these people signed a contract with House Carvaro, not the crown. And I'm sure I need not remind you who funds this expedition."

"An expedition currently traversing my father's road," Lyntia pointed out, stiffening in the saddle. "And bound by his laws. As are you, Ultria, as long as you abide within our borders."

Orsena's brows tightened in a manner Guyime hadn't seen before. Given the power she possessed, of which the princess was plainly ignorant, he found the expression concerning.

"Captain Guyime has my full confidence in commanding this army..." Orsena began, her frown deepening in annoyance when Guyime cut in.

"In point of fact, Ultria," he said, "there are sound reasons to proclaim Princess Lyntia the overall commander of this host. She is correct in pointing out the preponderance of Alcedonians in our ranks, a disparity that will only grow as we gather strength on the march. Also, I've often found that royal blood adds a necessary lustre to a leader, helps buttress the troops' courage to know they fight with the approval of one blessed by the gods themselves."

Orsena met his gaze, shifting a little in the saddle in a manner that told him she was hearing a taunt from the demon in her blade. This worried him more than her anger. A being such as her falling under a demon's influence would be a terrible thing indeed. He watched her perfect face exhibit a barely perceptible twitch before she mastered herself and returned her focus to the princess.

"I shall expect Captain Guyime to be consulted on all decisions," she said. "Also, the title of captain is insufficient. I prefer he be addressed henceforth as 'general'."

The Road of Storms

Lyntia, once again proving herself no fool, inclined her head with accustomed grace. "A fine arrangement, Ultria. Now, as you raise the subject of decisions, we have several to make. Chief amongst them being our intended line of march. All reports indicate that Rajan is leading his host directly towards the Pass of Armenion, which will place him on the Road of Storms in approximately three weeks. Whilst I believe it would be possible to force march a well-trained and disciplined army with sufficient speed to compel him to turn and give battle, this," she nodded to the untidy column raising dust on the northward road, "is not that."

"Rajan's host is larger than ours," Guyime said, "which makes it slower. However, I do not advise trying to catch him, but instead get ahead of him. You will recall that this expedition has two objectives, highness. First, the defeat of the Rebel King. Second, the recovery of the treasure of Nahossa. To do that, we must prevent him reaching the city before us."

"Get ahead of him?" Lyntia shook her head. "Impossible. There is but one viable route to the Road of Storms."

Guyime exchanged another glance with Orsena before offering a carefully phrased reply. "Amongst our party is one who possesses a remarkable gift for navigation. She believes she has found an alternate path."

"The Obsidian Cut?" Princess Lyntia gave a short, incredulous laugh as she surveyed the map set out before her. "Do you have any notion of what lies there, General?"

The map had been drawn by Lexius at Shavalla's direction. The privateer was a fair hand with the stylus, but the scholar possessed a level of skill beyond even the more accomplished cartographers. The chart depicted the mountains bordering Alcedon's northern provinces and the unerring straight line of the Road of Storms leading from the Pass of Armenion to Nahossa. Southeast of the pass, Lexius had drawn another, much shorter, straight line cutting through the peaks.

"It's the only way," Shavalla said, rolling her eyes and adding, "highness" in response to Guyime's glare. As was common amongst those who hailed from the Ice Veldt, she had little use for ceremony or the tedium of formal titles.

"And how could you know this?" Lyntia enquired. "Did it not occur to you that the Cut is shunned for good reason?" She stabbed a finger at the dotted line upon the map. "It's a place cursed by the gods. Obsidian cliffs so jagged they'll rip the skin off any hand that strays near them, home to a narrow ledge above a sheer drop with no bottom to it; at least none have ever seen and returned to speak of it. And the voices…" She trailed off into a shudder. "This is where you would have me lead my army?"

"I would, highness," Guyime stated, "that is, if you harbour any real hope of facing Rajan."

He spoke softly but was careful to emphasise his last word, taking satisfaction when he saw the barb sink home. The princess's aquiline features tightened as she concealed a wince, no doubt stung by the shame of defeat. Despite what he had told the recruits at the docks, Guyime was no stranger to lost battles and the injured pride they engendered. However, he had seen enough wars to know that allowing emotion to dictate a commander's decisions leads to calamity. Watching Lyntia's lips twitch as she continued to contemplate the map, it was clear she had yet to learn this lesson.

"I have walked this path," Lyntia went on, her voice softer now her gaze dark with grim recollection. "There are…things there. Things that can strip the courage from even the bravest soul."

"As my research confirms, highness," Lexius put in. "However, we believe we have a counter to such dangers."

Lyntia squinted at him. "What counter?"

Lexius hesitated, exchanging a glance with Guyime, speaking on when he received a nod. "To contest with magic, one must employ magic." His hand went to the pommel of the Kraken's Tooth. "Suffice to say, this company is experienced in its employment."

The doubt evident in the princess's frown faded only a little as she returned her attention to the chart. "You guarantee this will put us in Rajan's path?"

"Anyone who offers guarantees in war is a fool or a liar," Guyime replied. "But I will offer surety that if we do not take the Obsidian Cut there will be no prospect of bringing the Rebel King to battle."

Closing her eyes, the princess emitted a thin sigh. "Very well. However," turning, she cast a hard glare around the tent. "This course is to be concealed from the army, at least for now. There are some amongst my people who would forsake any amount of gold or silver rather than walk the Cut. I trust that's clear?"

Lexius and Lorweth had the sense to offer respectful bows, as did Anselm, although Guyime felt that the knight choosing to sink to one knee to be excessive. Orsena consented to incline her head whilst Shavalla could stir herself to no more than a shrug. Seeker, seated in a corner with the Morningstar cradled in her lap, gave no reaction at all.

Fortunately, Lyntia appeared more puzzled than offended by the disparity in formal respect. "We'll reach Ilzina tomorrow," she told Guyime. "It's a sizeable town and therefore likely to offer a decent haul of recruits. I trust you brought sufficient coin?"

"Of course, highness." Guyime offered her a bow of his own before she nodded and strode from the tent.

"Eyes up, lad," Shavalla said, tapping a finger to Anselm's head when she noticed how the knight's gaze lingered on the departing princess. "Royalty she may be, but trust me, you're far too good for her."

"She seeks to defend her people," Anselm returned, rising with a stiffened back. "Is that not to be admired?"

"It's not her courage you admire, but her fine-bred arse." Shavalla grinned in response to the knight's offended scowl. "Not easy to hide your feelings from those who carry a demon-cursed blade, laddie."

"Indeed," Anselm said, his jaw hardening. "Such as festering resentment towards one's betters."

Shavalla's grin blossomed into a laugh, although there was an edge to it. "Rest assured, I have no betters…"

"Can we get on?" Guyime's question brought a swift end to the burgeoning discord. He let the resulting silence linger, knowing the demons in each cursed blade would be communicating a chorus of dark suggestions. Guyime studied them, gauging their resistance. Lexius, of course, exhibited scant concern as the demon that had once inhabited the blade of the Kraken's Tooth had been displaced by the soul of Calandra, his sorceress wife. The others all betrayed some form of tension, the degree of which varied.

The Road of Storms

Shavalla was the most controlled, her mouth quirking in irritation rather than anger. Like Guyime, she had borne her sword for many years and had ample practice in resisting the Navigator's enticements. Outwardly, Anselm was the most distressed, flexing his hands to banish a tremble, whilst his features betrayed a range of poorly concealed emotions. Guyime knew this to result from the fact that his sword contained two warring spirits: the soul of Sir Lorent Athil locked in an endless contest with the death-worshipping Necromancer. Guyime didn't know how long his deceased comrade could sustain this struggle, for mortal souls will weary and fade over time. He could only hope that most valiant knight could hold out until they reached the Infernus Gate.

Orsena was the least affected, which, paradoxically, Guyime found to be the most concerning. Instead of grimacing in disgust, he saw her lower her face to conceal a smile, as if sharing a private joke with the Artisan.

Quite right, my liege, Lakorath affirmed. *When a demon makes you laugh, consider your soul half-claimed. You may well have to kill her before we even glimpse the Gate...if you can.*

"A war lies before us," Guyime said. "To win the Gate, we must win the war. All very unfortunate, but also unavoidable. To outward appearances, the princess holds sway, so make sure you maintain the appearance of dutiful captains."

"Captains?" Orsena asked.

"No army can march to the sound of but one voice. It must be organised, structured, and led accordingly. Anselm." The knight stiffened with dutiful attentiveness. "Besides the royal guards, I count nigh two hundred mounted fighters, mostly mercenaries. You will take charge of them, scout our routes and patrol our flanks. Hired swords can be a truculent bunch, so feel at liberty to administer any discipline you feel appropriate to ensure obedience.

"Shavalla," he went, turning to the privateer, "you will take charge of the other mercenaries. There's a good many sailors amongst them who'll respond well to the voice of a ship's captain."

"Faithless swabs who forsook their ships in hope of loot," Shavalla grunted in disdain. Seeing the hardness of Guyime's gaze, she raised her hands in surrender. "As you wish, old mate. Just don't be surprised when I have to flog a few."

"Seeker," Guyime said, causing the beast charmer to look up from the Morningstar. "Our archers are few in number, but still require a captain, if you're willing."

She met his gaze, her face betraying scant expression as she gave a nod, then returned her attention to the spiked ball in her lap.

Yes, Lakorath agreed, reading his thoughts. *You really should have tossed that fucking thing into the sea when you had the chance.*

"Lexius," Guyime said, moving on to the scholar. "You shall be our chief of intelligence. Anselm is bound to capture a few straggling rebels as we march north. Garner what information you can from them. I'll also need all the tales of the Guhltain you can recall. It seems likely we'll be facing not just one enemy on the Steppes."

"As you wish, my lord."

"Lorweth."

"Your worship?" Lorweth responded, his careful tone and surprised squint making it plain that he hadn't expected to receive a captaincy. "Not sure I'm best suited to soldiering of any sort. Certainly not the kind that requires all that standing straight and saluting business. Or the leading them into battle part of the job, truth be told. In point of fact, your worship, I think I'd rather avoid the whole enterprise altogether..."

"Rest easy," Guyime cut in. "I don't require you to lead, or soldier. Instead, I only ask that you do what you're good at."

"Which is?"

"Skulk, eavesdrop, ingratiate, and deceive." Guyime offered him a thin smile. "As this campaign wears on, it would be best to have ears and eyes amongst the troops. Listen to their gripes. Gauge their mood. I need to know how many of this lot will actually fight when battle dawns, as it surely will."

"And I?" Orsena asked, arching an eyebrow. "Have you no commission for me?"

"Every general needs an adjutant," Guyime replied. "One charged with ensuring the army is fed, supplies accounted for and rosters diligently kept. Since you opted to leave your consilio behind in Creztina, I think it only right the duty should fall to you, Ultria. You are paying for all of this, after all."

"I am. And the expense is certainly considerable. Yet, I'd spend every coin again to spare these poor souls what's coming. They are all going to perish before this is over. Are they not, your highness?"

"If the Infernus Gate opens, the chaos and suffering wreaked upon the world will be beyond all imagining. Set against that, the fate of one small army is nothing."

"It may be nothing to you, your highness." Guyime saw both guilt and resentment in the Ultria's expression, but also grim resignation. "I am not so accustomed to leading the destitute and desperate into annihilation."

"Well, if it's any comfort, my lady," Shavalla said, teeth shining white as she offered Orsena a broad smile, "we're all likely to perish with them, so at least we won't have to suffer the shame of our sin for long. Or maybe you will, being all indestructible and such."

Guyime expected an angry retort from the Ultria, but instead she merely let out a soft, sorrowful laugh. "One thing I have learned during this strange journey of ours," Orsena said. "Nothing is truly indestructible."

Chapter Five

THE NORTHWARD MARCH

•)———(•)———(•

The town of Ilzina came into view around noon the following day. A walled conurbation of white marble houses and towers topped with red tile roofs nestled amidst verdant fields, Guyime supposed it would have made for a pleasing sight if not for the fact it now stood a blackened ruin.

No recruits to be had here, my liege, Lakorath advised. *All I sense is death. The Rebel King is thorough, it seems.*

Close inspection proved the demon right. The narrow, cobbled streets of Ilzina were choked with corpses of all ages. Most had been hacked down, their bodies bearing gruesome evidence of ferocious slaughter. Some had died attempting to escape burning houses, their charred, stiffened limbs jutting from doorways and windows.

"Three days ago," Seeker advised. "Maybe four." Of them all, she possessed the most acute sense for signs left in the wake of death. "Little was stolen, so far as I can tell. A trail of bodies beyond the walls leads towards the west. Those who fled were cut down in the fields."

✦ 59 ✦

They had gathered about a well in the small square in the centre of the town. "They didn't spoil it," Lorweth said, water dripping from his face as he raised it from the bucket he had hauled from the well's depths. "A curious act for a rampaging army, wouldn't you say, your worship?"

"I assume his principal object was to deny us additional strength," Guyime said, eyes tracking over the slain littering the square. Wordless, pale-faced Alcedonian soldiers wandered amongst them, some seeking kin, most just lost in the numbness that results from witnessing so great a crime. "And sowing fear."

"This is..." Princess Lyntia began, then faltered to silence. Her features held much the same blankness as her countrymen, though Guyime spied a burgeoning wetness to her eyes. Noting his scrutiny, her face hardened and she blinked the moisture away. "This is unlike him," she said, coughing to dispel the hoarseness in her voice.

"The Rebel King doesn't murder?" Guyime asked.

"Oh, he's done murder aplenty, but not like this. Never the innocent. The villages he destroyed during his march to Creztina were empty, the folk who dwelt there driven off before the torches were thrown. Never before did he indulge in such wanton carnage."

Guyime met Seeker's eye, seeing a shared conclusion: this was the Desecrator's doing, which meant the order for the massacre had been given in Ekiri's voice.

"We can expect more of this on the road north," Guyime told the princess. "At least until we turn towards the Obsidian Cut. The hired blades amongst us are accustomed to such sights, whilst many of your people are not. It would be best if they were not permitted to enter any other places subject to such destruction. For the sake of morale, you understand, highness."

"These are my people," Lyntia responded. "I'll spare my army the sight of such ugliness, but not myself. At the very least, a princess of this realm should mark their passing with an offering to the gods."

Accordingly, she summoned the small coterie of priests accompanying the army to conduct a short ceremony. They erected a small altar in the square before which the princess knelt whilst the clerics sang incantations in an ancient tongue as they wafted smoke from vessels of burning incense. It mixed with the stench of rotting and charred bodies to create a yet more foul miasma that Guyime felt to be far from divine.

I have never met a god, Lakorath mused as Guyime retreated from the scene, eyes stinging. *And find it curious that mortals always assume them to be so fond of powerful aromas. Is the great stink of humanity not enough, I wonder?*

Guyime was well used to the demon's disdain for mortal kind, yet detected a keener edge of loathing in Lakorath's shared thoughts than was usual. "If you detest us so," he said, "why assist me in frustrating the Desecrator's design?"

Because his victory will also be demon-kind's defeat, my liege. He will make slaves of us all, and I have lived far too long in this metal prison to abide yet more bondage. Besides, with the Desecrator vanquished in accordance with Arkelion's wishes, the enchantment that binds me will vanish. I shall, at last, be free.

"And what, pray tell, will you do with such freedom?"

The demon responded with a long, hearty laugh, but said no more.

Come the evening, it transpired that the Rebel King's intent on depriving the army of fresh recruits had been mistaken, at least in part. After the host encamped for the night, the pickets began reporting a steady influx of people from the surrounding fields. Some came in search of food, but most sought an audience with the princess so that they might offer their strength to her cause.

"I was out working the fields when they came, highness." The man who knelt before Lyntia named himself Harelion of Ilzina. Middling in age but impressive of stature, he clutched a woodsman's axe in one hand and placed the other over his heart as he spoke. Guyime knew this to be the custom in Alcedon when the speaker wished it known that they uttered only truth and would suffer the gods' wrath for a lie. Arrayed behind him was a cluster of bedraggled folk, mostly young, clutching scythes and sundry bladed implements. They were poorly clothed and besmirched, but Guyime recognised the glint in the eyes of all: the hunger for retribution.

"We didn't know what was happening 'til we saw the smoke." Harelion paused, his heavy jaw working as he swallowed a sob. "The scum had all moved on by the time we got there. My wife and little 'uns… My old ma and pa too…"

He subsided into choking grief, lowering his head further until Lyntia stepped forward to rest a hand on his head. "Be not ashamed of your sorrow, good man Harelion. Cherish it, for it honours those you have lost. As will your service, should you choose to give it."

Letting out a gasp, Harelion took up his axe in both hands, raising it in offering. "Command us, highness! We are yours!"

With a grave smile, Lyntia traced her fingers over the man's tear-streaked face. "Gladly and with gratitude, I shall. General Guyime!"

"Highness!" Guyime stepped forward smartly, offering her a low bow.

"I hereby name this man Captain Harelion of a company to be known henceforth as the Blades of Ilzina. Please ensure he and his soldiers are provisioned and armed. He will also be present at all future councils."

Guyime bowed again. "I shall see to it, highness."

"Rise now, Captain," Lyntia told Harelion, gently guiding him to his feet before addressing her next words to his fellow townsfolk. "I cannot replace all you have lost. But I can promise reward for loyal service and that most precious thing, justice. Will you follow me and claim it?"

The subsequent collective shout was as rich in savage intent as any Guyime had heard from vengeful throats. Watching Lyntia step forward to embrace the yelling crowd, seeing the mix of bloodlust and adulation on their faces, it occurred to him that he had underestimated the princess's abilities.

"She only lost because she faced the Warlord," he murmured in realisation, receiving a confirmatory sigh from Lakorath.

Quite so, my liege. But I'm starting to suspect I know the identity of the demon in the Warlord's Tulwar, and if I'm right, he has never tasted defeat in battle. The moment the two of you meet will be very interesting indeed.

s Guyime had predicted, their path was strewn with the ugly evidence of the rebel host's passing. Village after village lay in ruins, corpses plentiful amongst the blackened dwellings, but so were the vengeful volunteers who continued to appear whenever the Royal Host halted. Soon, there was enough for another company under another captain, a hefty woman named Euricia with features set in a permanent rictus of hate. Unlike Harelion, she shed no tears when kneeling before Princess Lyntia, but Guyime didn't doubt the truth in the oath she gave to spare none in the princess's cause.

According to Orsena's tally of the army's strength, it had grown to near eight thousand by the time they reached the point where the road branched into an unpaved track leading towards the northeast. The rate of desertion was also far below Guyime's expectations, amounting to only a few dozen since departing Creztina. He ascribed this partly to the soldiers' patent fear of his wrath, deepened when he made good on his promised floggings after Anselm's cavalry captured the first few deserters. However, he knew true credit for the army's cohesion lay not with their general, but their princess.

During the day's march, Lyntia paced alongside the column on her black warhorse, calling out encouragement to stragglers. Come evening she toured the camp, moving from fire to fire and exchanging good-humoured banter with those who dared speak to her. Guyime had once done much the same, but never had the Ravager enjoyed so easy a rapport with his troops. Even amongst those who followed his banner, fear of the hate-filled man who wore an ensorcelled blade had always been the dominant sentiment. Lyntia was not feared, she was loved, and the reason was not hard to divine; she loved them back.

THE ROAD OF STORMS

Troubling, my liege, Lakorath warned as Guyime watched the princess share a wineskin with a cluster of recent recruits. *Can she be compelled to sacrifice what she loves to secure her vengeance?*

Guyime didn't voice his reply, but the demon surely heard the bitter, guilt-laden thought that formed it. *Why not? I did.*

The turn towards the northeast spared the army the horror of bearing daily witness to the rebel horde's crimes, but brought a halt to the steady flow of recruits. Anselm reported the route to the Obsidian Cut free of enemies and thinly populated. It wasn't hard to see why. The further north they marched, the less verdant the surrounding terrain. Green fields, orchards, and vineyards gave way to rocky, sparsely forested hills. Also, the dust grew thicker by the mile, so that when, after another week's march, the wind began to take on a chilly edge and the sky spill ever more frequent torrents of rain, Guyime counted it a relief.

When the mountains crested the northern horizon, he convinced Lyntia to reduce the number of miles marched each day in favour of increasing the hours of drill in the evening. "Every step towards the north brings us closer to battle, highness," he advised. "Something most of our number have never seen. We should do all we can to ready them."

The princess was happy to leave the daily chore of training in the hands of Guyime and his captains. A shrewd decision since it spared her the resentment inevitably aroused by such tedious labour. Standard Alcedonian weaponry consisted of a seven-foot spear, round shield, and short sword, complemented by a breastplate and greaves of bronze or leather. But, thanks to the mismatched nature of this army, only about half possessed the full set of soldierly accoutrements. Consilio Evehla had shown typical foresight in including a decent supply of additional weapons and armour in the baggage train, but that had all been swiftly absorbed by the vengeful recruits. Consequently, at least half had nothing more by way of arms than a scythe, hatchet, or pitchfork. Many possessed only a knife, and some no blade at all. These Guyime armed with clubs hewn from trees, studding them with nails supplied by the army's ever busy band of smiths. The clubbers, as they were swiftly dubbed by the rest of the army, he gathered into small detachments a few dozen strong. When battle joined, he would place them behind the main line, charged with rushing forward to plug any gaps.

Given what Lexius had told him of the Guhltain's tactics, he concentrated on teaching the better armed cohorts the tricky art of rapidly forming a circular spear hedge. The formation was a tried and tested means of staving off a massed cavalry charge, with the soldiers overlapping shields to protect against the inevitable attentions of circling horse archers. For the most part, the recruits took to the hours of forming, breaking, and reforming ranks with a diligence that would have aroused envy in his younger self. Lorweth's regular reports on their mood also buttressed the sense of soldiers unified by a grim sense of purpose, with notable exceptions.

"It's the hired blades who moan the loudest, your worship," the druid said. "Those attuned to war have a nose for when things aren't right. Many have heard dire tales of the Guhltain and don't fancy a trip across the Steppes on foot with so little cavalry to guard the flanks. Shavalla does her best to keep them in check, and the sailors amongst them will surely follow her anywhere. The veteran fighters, however, owe allegiance to but one thing." Lorweth rubbed his forefinger and thumb together. "A bit more persuading wouldn't go amiss. If her ladyship has any gold left to offer, that is."

Knowing well the consequences of dealing with mutinous sellswords, Guyime took the druid's advice to heart. Although it chafed on his disciplinary instincts, especially after his unambiguous speech in Creztina, the next day he asked Orsena to visit the mercenary camp with an offer of revised terms: all who gave a solemn oath to see this campaign to the end would receive a lifetime contract with House Carvaro. The prospect of guaranteed future employment and a comfortable retirement was something few hired blades could ever aspire to, and sufficed to quell the misgivings of the majority. A dozen or so, still fearful of facing the Guhltain on the open steppe, slipped away before the next dawn. Anselm pleaded for leave to pursue the faithless wretches, but Guyime refused him. Hunting them down would surely lead to a skirmish. This army had reached the peak of its strength and he wouldn't risk one more drop of its blood than necessary.

Another potential counter to the horse tribes of the Sunless Steppes lay with Seeker's archers. The contingent had doubled in size during the march, swollen by hunters from the ravaged country left in the Rebel King's wake. Additional reinforcement came from a few dozen slingers, use of this inexpensive but effective weapon being a long-standing custom in the farmlands of Alcedon.

Guyime found Seeker crouched with the slingers amongst the rocks fringing the western edge of the camp. Seeing him approach, she put a finger to her lips and motioned for him to lower himself. Doing so, Guyime waited, watching the fading sun paint a red hue across the stunted trees covering the slope below. Somewhere amidst the forest, a shout echoed and a mass of quail rose from the trees. When the flock ascended high enough to be silhouetted against the sunset, the slingers loosed their stones. He saw bird after bird tumble from the sky before the chirping cloud streaked overhead and scattered across the hills.

"Feel at leave to join us, Pilgrim," Seeker said, reaching down to gather up a quail. Broken wing flapping, it emitted a constant, high-pitched trill until she snapped its neck. "We have meat aplenty."

Seeker's cohort were a mostly silent bunch, clustered around their fires to share the feast of roasted birds with none of the ribald chatter or song-singing common to encamped armies. He noted the way their eyes strayed constantly to their captain, tense with expectation, as if ready to spring to action at her slightest command. This was not the loyalty born of mutual regard enjoyed by Princess Lyntia, but a blind, unnatural devotion Guyime knew arose from a different source.

The Morningstar sat at Seeker's side, emitting a faint, pulsating glow from the lettering inscribing the metal. Not for the first time, Guyime was seized by a fierce desire to be rid of it. Perhaps Lexius could conjure a bolt from the Kraken's Tooth powerful enough to melt the thing into slag. But the notion supposed that Seeker would sit idly by and watch, and he knew she wouldn't.

"Does it…talk?" Guyime ventured. "Have you heard voices, whispers in your mind?"

THE ROAD OF STORMS

Seeker's gaze slid towards him as she continued to turn the brace of spitted quail over the fire. "No," she said. Guyime saw an angry crease to her brow but also a stiffness to her movements that spoke of rigid self control.

"I know what it is, Pilgrim," she added. "I know why you fret over me like a worrisome wolf over a cub. Know that it did not claim me. I claimed it."

"Be that as it may." He cast a meaningful glance towards the surrounding archers and slingers. "It seems to have claimed them, much as it once claimed the Black Reaver's pirates."

"You wanted me to lead." Seeker tested the flesh of a bird with her fingers, grunted in satisfaction, then extended the spit to offer it to Guyime. "And so I do. Given our goal, does the manner of my leadership matter?"

"It'll matter to your soldiers." Taking a dagger from his belt, he jabbed it into the bird, lifting it clear of the spit. "Or does their fate not concern you?"

"You know, there has long been only one soul whose fate concerns me, and it is not my own. I have followed you across countless miles through the worst dangers, Pilgrim. And to save Ekiri, I'd do so again a thousand times. This," she placed a hand on the haft of the Morningstar, "will be the means by which I wrest her from his grasp. With this, I know I can fight my way to her side, and when I do, when she looks at last into the face of her mother, not even a lord of the Infernus will keep her from me."

Chapter Six

THE OBSIDIAN CUT

Viewed from afar, the Obsidian Cut seemed an overly grandiose name for what appeared to be a dark scar upon the white and grey majesty of the north Alcedonian mountains. Princess Lyntia had revealed their course to the army the night before. The entire host had been arrayed below a suitably steep rise so that she could address them as one.

"By now you know my words as truth," she told them, voice echoing across the ranks. "And so, when I say this is the only course that will bring us victory and the justice we crave, I shall trust that you believe me. I have walked this path before. In my youth when I lusted for adventure and, in my folly, scorning the sage advice of elders, I walked the Obsidian Cut. I lived to tell the tale, but will not pretend to you that it holds no danger. Peril there is aplenty upon that dark road, but walk it we must." She raised her fist above her head, calling out the three words that had become the army's mantra. "Victory and justice!"

They had responded with fulsome enthusiasm at the time, chanting their response with spears stabbing the air. Yet, as he scanned the pale, wide-eyed faces of the soldiers

❖ 71 ❖

trooping towards the Cut, Guyime wondered if their collective desire for retribution would sustain them against so deep a pitch of fear.

"If you would be so kind, highness," Guyime said, watching Lyntia staring hard and long at the dark, narrow notch cut into the mountains, "I should like to know more of the nature of the threat we face here."

"Haven't you heard of it?" she asked, not turning from her vigil. "I thought the tale famed throughout the Five Seas."

In fact, Guyime recalled only vague allusions to a best avoided mountain pass during his last sojourn through Alcedon. Lexius had provided some additional details but, unusually, confessed that much regarding the origin and nature of the Obsidian Cut lay outside his ken.

"It's a relic of the Kraken Wars," Guyime said. "The result of some magical foulness conjured by an Ultrean Wizard King seeking to destroy the Valkerin legions sent against his final redoubt."

"So some say," Lyntia acceded. "But there are other tales. Some hold that a fissure opened between this world and Akrius, the hidden realm whence the gods consign only the worst souls, allowing their malignity to seep into the mountains. Others claim that my ancestors beseeched the gods to carve them a new route to the Sunless Steppes, an alternative to the always watched Pass of Armenion. Instead, ever capricious, the overlords of the High Realm crafted a path any sane commander would avoid lest they lose their army entire."

"Yet you have walked it and survived to tell the tale."

"Yes, I have walked it. But no, I've never told the tale. I did not set out upon the path alone, General. Yet, I returned so."

Lyntia turned to regard Lexius perched atop a wagon nearby, doubt evident in her frown. "A small man," she said. "But wielder of great power, at least so you promise. I'll confess I didn't take him for a mighty sorcerer capable of crafting a spell that can shield an entire army from fear."

In fact, the spell was Calandra's, but Guyime had opted against informing the princess that their fate depended on a mortal soul trapped in an ancient sword. Thus far, she had shown a remarkable trust in her general and his strange companions, but he felt revealing the truth of the demon-cursed blades might be asking for more than she could offer.

"Of all those who walk at my side," Guyime said, "he is the one I trust without question. He will see us through, highness."

"As I understand the particulars of your scholar's spell," Lyntia had said to the assembled captains that night, "it will spare us the terror that infects the minds of all who enter the Obsidian Cut, but not what you see and hear there." She hesitated, swallowing a cough. "Which is unfortunate. Remember at all times that they are phantoms, no more real than a dream, regardless of how substantial they seem or how much truth they speak. Ensure all in your charge are warned in the strongest terms to pay them no heed. They must focus their mind only on the next step, then the step after that."

Now, as Guyime stood with her before the vast triangle of the Cut's southern opening, he wondered if any enchantment, no matter how powerful, could banish the fear inherent in this place. At a distance, it possessed a gleaming quality, giving the impression of a smooth, shiny passage through the irregular granite edifice of the mountains. Now Guyime saw that to be false. The walls of black glass were jagged. Every inch featured a spiky protrusion that Lyntia assured them would draw blood at the slightest touch. More disconcerting was its stark artificiality. There were no curves to the Obsidian Cut, its far reaches stretching off into misted obscurity. It was as if a gargantuan scalpel blade had descended from the sky to deliver a precise incision all the way to the Sunless Steppes. The sense of a thing fashioned by design rather than nature was enhanced by the ledge. Ten feet wide, utterly flat, and tracing the length of the Cut, it could accommodate the passage of the entire army, including wagons. However, the absence of any barrier protecting against a fall into the sheer drop to the left of the walkway instilled an inescapable, instinctive dread.

Lyntia insisted on leading the host into the glass chasm. Taking hold of her horse's reins, she nodded to Lexius to begin his work. Drawing the Kraken's Tooth, the scholar briefly held the flickering blade before his eyes. "We stand ready, my love," he murmured, whereupon the steel took on a far brighter glow. Lexius held the blade out, pointing it into the Cut as it shone with ever more energy. Forced to shield his eyes, Guyime realised there was more to this spell than luminosity. He could feel a shift in the air, a mounting pressure accompanied by a certain dullness of sensation. He only dimly felt his hand upon his brow, but the spell went beyond touch. He found the worries that had beset him throughout this march abruptly quelled. Seeker's attachment to the Morningstar, Orsena's growing affection for her demon, and the myriad annoyances that came with commanding an army. Suddenly, they felt distant, almost inconsequential.

A shout from Lexius compelled Guyime to lower his hand from his eyes, seeing the scholar stagger as a pulse of light blasted from the Kraken's Tooth. It swept along the Obsidian Cut, banishing the mist to reveal its unerringly straight length in full. As it progressed, it left traces of itself upon the jagged walls of the great chasm, small, glittering points of light that resembled a star field called to earth.

"It should last until nightfall, highness," Lexius informed the princess with a bow. "Though, I regret that I cannot give assurance that all who march with this army will be immune to terror. For some, the fear they carry is so great, no magic can banish it."

The princess nodded in grave acknowledgement, then started forward. "Then let us not tarry." Her voice was steady, but so tightly controlled in pitch that Guyime was compelled to wonder if her own fear was of a scale beyond the reach of Calandra's spell.

For the first hour, nothing of note happened. Guyime led his grey mare in Lyntia's wake, casting frequent glances back at the ranks trooping along behind. The ledge's flatness denied him a full view of the soldiers arrayed in three-file order. When he toured the camp the night before, he had seen many drawing lots or throwing dice to decide who would occupy the outer file. The absence of shouts or other discord succoured the notion that the spell was holding and they might enjoy an untroubled passage. However, with each passing mile, it became plain that Lyntia's warnings regarding this place were not fanciful.

He saw the phantom before he heard it, a flicker of grey hovering at the edge of his vision. He resisted the impulse to turn his head, but from the troubled murmur rippling through the ranks behind, not all had heeded their princess's injunction. The voice came as the phantom drifted closer, invading more of Guyime's sight, though he strove to keep his gaze upon the plodding hooves of Lyntia's charger. "Was I not a good son, Father?" the phantom enquired, its voice a pitiful rasp but possessing a horrible familiarity. "Is that why you killed me?"

Unwilling to behold the face he would see if he were to alter his gaze even a little, Guyime clenched his jaw and began to count the falls of the charger's hooves. He stopped at ten, then started over in the hope that repetition would blot out the phantom's terrible enticements.

"One, two, three, four…"

"Have you no words for me, Father? Have you no tears for the son you sacrificed upon the altar of your vengeance? Was it worth it, I wonder? It's so cold here, Father. This place you sent me to. It *so* cold…"

"…five, six, seven…"

"I am made to watch her die, Father. Again and again, they torment me with the sight of Loise's death. I smell her hair burning… Her flesh…"

"Eight!" The numbers hissed through gritted teeth as Guyime continued to force them out. He was dimly aware of shouts and screams to his rear, but dared not turn. "Nine! Ten!"

"Have you no words for me?" The phantom's voice took on an accusatory edge, the grey face fluttering before Guyime's eyes. "No comfort for the son you murdered? Had I lived, would I not have been a prince? A king to be. Perhaps, in time, it would have been I who murdered you, for power is such a seductive thing..."

It was this that banished the illusion. Guyime stopped counting and finally turned to confront the spectre. His fear had gone, though a residue of anger remained. The face before him was a decent facsimile of Ellipe's youthful features, but the malicious half-sneer it wore added to its falsity.

"I know not what you are," Guyime told it. "But my son could never raise a hand to me, nor would his heart have ever been twisted by the lure of power. Get you hence, spirit, and trouble me no more."

The spectre's sneer deepened. A cackle, rich in malice and hunger issued from a mouth that had widened into a dark maw. "Such hatred," it hissed, looming closer. The confluence of grey tendrils that formed it took on a darker pitch, the shadowed aperture of its gaping mouth, but the voice continued. "Hatred for yourself. Always so much more of a delight to savour..."

"Is this a dream wraith?" Guyime asked Lakorath, putting a hand to the Nameless Blade as the coiling shadow lunged for him.

No, the demon replied in a laconic muse. *I believe it to be something else.*

"Be precise!" Guyime snapped, the sword flashing free of the scabbard on his back to slash at the phantom. It was quick, however, swerving aside so that only the blade's tip caught a trailing tendril. Apparently, even that minor touch sufficed to inflict grievous pain. The thing let out a screech loud enough to echo to the depths of the chasm below, recoiling from Guyime like an injured snake.

Unless I'm mistaken, it's a facet of a curse, Lakorath continued. *Placed upon the Obsidian Cut long ago. There's a whiff of shamanic blood magic to it. The princess's story about this place being an attempt by her forebears to carve a new path to the Sunless Steppes is probably correct. In turn, the Guhltain's ancestors concocted a curse to block it. Something powerful enough to endure this long would require a monumental sacrifice. Hundreds, perhaps thousands, of throats slit and the souls of the dead consigned here to feast upon the hatred and fear of the living. An impressive achievement. But, as you can see, no match for demonic power.*

The spectre Guyime had wounded continued to twist and howl, shedding parts of itself all the while. Glancing back along the line, Guyime saw the first few ranks in disarray. Soldiers crowded against the walls of the Cut, faces stark with fear as more phantoms assailed them. To Guyime's eyes, the spectres seemed uniform in nature, each one a shifting cluster of shadow. But he knew every soldier saw a singular face from their past, something concocted to drag forth the poison from the darkest recesses of their souls. From further down the line, Guyime heard the despairing wail of a man plummeting into the chasm and knew he wouldn't be the last.

"Pay them no heed!" Lyntia shouted. Coming to Guyime's side, features drawn in anguish, she pleaded with her soldiers, heedless of the spectre looming at her back. Guyime sliced it in two with an overhead swipe of the Nameless Blade, the thing's scream paining his ears as its remnants twisted in the air.

"Close your eyes!" Lyntia implored the cowering soldiers, the cries of yet more casting themselves into the chasm echoing along the Cut. "They are figments! They can only harm you if you let them!"

THE ROAD OF STORMS

Her words had little effect on the troops, the disordered ranks convulsing as fear took hold. Stepping forward, Guyime shredded a phantom with a flourish of steel, but the others merely retreated out of reach, continuing to cast their terror upon the soldiers.

Try this, my liege, Lakorath said, and Guyime noted a sudden increase in the glow of the Nameless Blade. "Shield your eyes, highness," he advised Lyntia before extending the sword and averting his own gaze. A heartbeat later, the steel, now shining brighter than the sun, unleashed a pulse of blue luminescence. Through watering eyes, Guyime saw the expanding light tear all the phantoms in sight to pieces, leaving only coiling black flecks drifting like ash after a quenched fire. The nearby troops sagged in mingled relief and confusion as the terror of seconds before faded with jarring suddenness. However, the screams sounding from their rear indicated their troubles were far from over.

"Tell the others," Guyime instructed Lakorath, the blade flickering as its occupant communicated with its fellow demons. Soon, flares of unleashed demon magic lit the Cut, the shrieks of the destroyed phantoms supplanting those of the unfortunates they had driven to suicide. Guyime waited until the last cries faded before sheathing the sword and turning to Lyntia.

"I believe it's safe to proceed now, highness," he said.

Her gaze shifted from his face to the sword on his back, shrewd eyes narrowed in contemplation. Her well-informed brother had surely known that Orsena's party carried enchanted weaponry. Given the calculation on Lyntia's brow, he suspected the prince had chosen not to share the truth of how much power they wielded.

Blinking, she stiffened her back and shifted her attention to the soldiers. They sagged in mingled confusion and relief, many weeping with the horrors they had witnessed lingering on their faces. "Straighten up, there!" their princess barked. "We've still miles to march this day."

Chapter Seven

UPON THE ROAD OF STORMS

•)———(•)———(•

The Sunless Steppes remained one of the few places within the orbit of the Five Seas Guyime had not yet walked. Gazing out across a landscape lacking features save an occasional undulation or slight change in hue of the perennial yellow-green grass, he felt scant regret at the omission. The sky was an incessant panoply of grey and black cloud, occluding sunlight apart from an infrequent glimmer that sent a patch of brightness drifting over the plains, always short-lived.

"The Graveyard of all Armies, my grandfather called it," Lyntia commented. "Never truly conquered, nor mapped in its entirety, since the Guhltain will slaughter even those who come in peace bearing no weapons."

"A map *is* a weapon, highness," Guyime replied. "As I fancy the Guhltain know full well."

Lyntia snorted a short laugh of agreement as she scanned the northern horizon. "There," she said, extending a finger. "See it?"

Since departing the Obsidian Cut, lessened in number by the two hundred souls who had cast themselves into the chasm, the army had marched across this sea of grass for three days. In that time Guyime had glimpsed nothing that could be termed a landmark. Following Lyntia's finger, he squinted at the distant join betwixt land and sky until his eyes detected an interruption in the wavering line. Although rendered small by the distance, he could tell this was the summit of a very tall structure.

"What is it?" he asked.

"A god," she replied. "Every fifth mile of the Road of Storms is marked by a mighty statue to a different god. They increase in size and importance the closer one draws to Nahossa. This will be one of the middling deities."

When the first statue came fully into view, Guyime could only wonder at the dimensions of the more salient Alcedonian gods. Depicting a confluence of woman and snake, the monument rose to a height of sixty feet or more. Lyntia named her Emystra, the divinity charged with the punishment of blasphemous mortals. Her beauteous head and torso rested atop a building-sized plinth, about which her serpentine lower half was coiled. The goddess's head was angled so that she stared down at the road below, her features carved into an expression of sorrowful contemplation.

"Emystra's punishments were terrible," Lyntia explained, "but she had been cursed with a kind heart, so suffered grievous pain whenever her fellow gods demanded she perform her duties. The priests hold that her tale is a lesson in the nature of justice. To work, it must be cruel, but also administered by those who understand its cruelty."

The Road of Storms

The road itself was a cracked and wasted track. The paving that had once covered it all the way to the divine city was mostly dust and grit now, yet the arrow straightness of its course gave testament to a once-impressive feat of engineering.

"The road crumbled but the statues remain," Lexius observed, enlarged eyes bright as he gazed up at Emystra's mournful stone features. "So many centuries of wind and rain, yet I see scant sign of degradation."

"A long-pondered mystery, master scholar," Lyntia told him with a smile. Guyime had noted that, of all his companions, only Lexius appeared capable of arousing any true sign of regard. Anselm's attempts at chivalric flattery had earned him little more than a guarded nod. Shavalla and Lorweth received only curt instruction, whilst the princess did consent to gild her words a little when addressing Orsena. Still, the resentment behind her eyes was obvious. With Guyime, she displayed more willingness towards conversation, but her suspicion lingered, and deepened after his display in the Cut. For Lexius, however, her demeanour was that of a high status noble engaging with a fondly esteemed counsellor.

"The works of mortal kind fade, but the divine does not," she went on. "To the priests, the undying monuments to the gods are evidence of their eternal divinity, and who is to say they are wrong?"

They encamped for the night beneath Emystra's regretful gaze, Guyime ordering a double watch kept after the nightly drills. Although Lexius's reports on the favoured tactics of the Guhltain indicated they would wait to gather strength before launching an attack, Guyime still expected them to at least mount a reconnaissance. Curiously, the night passed with the picket line untroubled and Lakorath sensing no living souls upon the surrounding plains save a few hawks and rabbits.

Come the morning, Guyime told Anselm to divide his company, sending the knight with one contingent to scout the south and the other ranging to the north. If their stratagem had worked, the Rebel King's horde would be behind them by several miles, but he was fully aware that they faced more than one foe upon these plains. The advent of noon, however, brought grim tidings from both directions.

"The road is clear, sire," Anselm stated. "We found tracks aplenty that told of the passage of a large force, and close to three hundred bodies strewn along the route. None had fallen to battle, so far as could be told. This," he grimaced and gestured to the sword on his back, "avowed that they had expired from exhaustion and want of sustenance."

"The bugger's got ahead of us," Lorweth concluded with a bitter laugh, and Guyime couldn't find fault with his reasoning.

"It appears Rajan must have driven his horde to supreme efforts, highness," he informed a stern-faced Lyntia shortly afterwards. Around them, the army was already breaking camp, the air filled with the shouted orders of captains and sergeants. "Beyond the endurance of many who follow his banner. Though it's likely he still possesses considerable strength."

"Meaning the lives we lost in the Cut were for nothing," the princess said, voice as hard as flint.

"Our tactic didn't have its intended effect, it is true. However, we still saved many days on the march and are much closer to the enemy than we would otherwise have been had we not taken the Cut. In part, the Rebel King's tactic works to our favour. Every mile he drives his army on it costs him strength, meaning we will face a greatly weakened foe once we close the distance."

"Assuming we can do so, or that the Guhltain will leave us be in the meantime."

"A forced march is never to be relished, highness, but I see no alternative here. A disciplined army can march thirty miles in a day, more if pushed."

"And a hundred miles separates us from Nahossa. You would have me waste my own strength too? This host has already suffered from my orders. I'll not add deathly exhaustion to their burden. Fortunately, Nahossa is a city that, by its nature, cannot be easily fortified. Rajan may beat us to the treasure, but he'll have no time to carry it off. With his forces so tired, he will be ripe for attack."

Guyime paused, uncertain of what lies he should tell. The princess's grasp of the situation was sound, in strict military terms, had their object merely been to secure nonexistent riches. How to persuade her of the necessity of reaching Nahossa before the Desecrator could open the Infernus Gate?

I regret I have only my previous counsel to offer, my liege, Lakorath interjected. *Kill her and take the army. Wait until nightfall, then a quiet neck snapping should do the trick. Say she fell off her horse or something.*

Guyime's quandary was temporarily forestalled by the arrival of the northward scouting party. It was led by a scarfaced stable master from Ilzina, who swiftly leapt from the saddle to kneel before Lyntia with head lowered. "Forgive the interruption, highness," he gasped from a dust-choked throat, "but my tidings are most urgent."

"Out with them, then," Lyntia said with an impatient flick of her wrist.

"The Guhltain, highness." The stable master paused to spit and drag more air into his lungs. "Upon the road ahead."

"They always did have the most impeccable timing," the princess muttered, exchanging a glance with Guyime before turning back to the kneeling scout. "What's their strength, man?"

"Well." The stable master darted a look at Lyntia's face, his expression the wary grimace of one who suspects he won't be believed. "The thing is, highness, they're all dead. Every one of them."

The bodies lay in a rough circle two miles wide around the base of another statue. It possessed the body of a man and the head and wings of an eagle, standing in magisterial indifference to the carnage that surrounded it. Lyntia named this one as Turha, the Warden of the Skies, though she was too distracted by the sprawled dead to offer any elaboration on his legend.

The first corpse they came to consisted of a horse and rider. From the nature of their wounds, Guyime judged them to have fallen to spear thrusts. The rider was a man of tanned, weathered features, clad in a jerkin of thick fur, stained dark where it had been pierced in several places. An empty sabre scabbard hung at his belt and a strong bow and quiver full of arrows was strapped to his saddle.

"Lost his blade and didn't loose a single arrow," Shavalla concluded, head angled as she studied the body. "I'd take him for a coward if all his wounds weren't in his chest rather than his back."

"He was certainly lost to terror at the moment of his death," Anselm said. It transpired that the Necromancer's Glaive possessed the ability to sense the emotions lingering in the recently slain. "A fear so great he couldn't even flee when they bore him down."

Not all the fallen were Guhltain. Clustered around the statue's feet, they found a pile of corpses clad in the kilts and woollen fleeces of Alcedonian northerners. The slashes and puncture wounds they bore provided testament to a truly ferocious close quarter struggle.

"Less fear in evidence here," Anselm advised, as he wandered amongst the dead. "Still it abides, like a stink that won't fade."

Guyime turned to Orsena and swept his arm about the field. "What's your reckoning?"

"Ten thousand at least," she said after a moment of sombre calculation. "I'd say a quarter of them were rebels."

"If the Guhltain lost over seven thousand warriors here, their host must be much larger," Lyntia mused.

"Your pardon, highness," Anselm said with a low bow, "but I am compelled to disagree. From the…sense of this place, I discern a shared lineage amongst the slain horse-folk. I believe they were all of one clan, an ancient bloodline that now lies extinguished upon this field."

"What a curiously discerning eye you have, sir," Lyntia observed, casting a pointed glance at the blade on Anselm's back. However, she didn't find fault with his conclusion, despite her mystified scowl. "Seven thousand attacking a force five times their strength. The Guhltain are never lacking in courage, but this speaks of foolishness."

"They are famed for winning victories against superior numbers," Guyime said. "And look here." He kicked a blackened stick lying on the ground, one of many littering the battlefield. "Torches. I believe the Guhltain attacked under cover of night, trusting to surprise and superior skill to win the day. Against a less well-prepared enemy, it might have worked."

"And the fear Anselm spoke of?" Seeker asked. From the tension in her face, Guyime could tell she already knew his answer.

"She's done it before," he pointed out. "Remember the guards at Iron Shield Pass? This…" He cast a grim eye around the scene. "Would indicate her powers have grown. My reading is that the Guhltain attacked in two wings from opposite directions. Ekiri… the Desecrator sent a wave of fear at the larger wing, sowing confusion and allowing them to be cut down with relative ease. The smaller wing managed to fight their way here, but had not the numbers to win anything but their own destruction."

"The power to terrorise an opposing army," Orsena said, wincing. "Not a thing to relish, or be easily countered."

"Enough!" The snap of the princess's voice brought an abrupt end to the discussion. She surveyed them all in turn, the suspicion on her brow supplanted by burgeoning understanding. "The witch. That's who you're talking about. Am I wrong?"

Guyime began to answer, but she held up a hand.

"I believe, my loyal captains," Lyntia said, "it is time for a fulsome explanation as to who exactly you are, what is the nature of the swords you carry, and why you are pursuing a foreign witch with such ardent fervour. And, mark you well, I do not wish to hear any more horse shit about treasure."

The Road of Storms

The firelight painted Lyntia's features a soft shade of yellow as she sat contemplating all she had been told. She had consented to wait upon their unexpurgated story until the army completed a gruelling day's march. Guyime and his captains hectored the plodding ranks past another four towering statues until he judged the soldiers close to the limit of their endurance. He reckoned they had covered a little over twenty miles of road, feeling it a decent distance for a non-veteran army. Come nightfall, they encamped beneath the tallest statue yet. Unlike the previous gods, this one featured no animalistic embellishment. Instead, the ancient blocks of shaped granite formed a mighty human warrior, bearing both shield and spear, his features hidden by the helm he wore. This, the princess informed them, was Mynaeon, the Alcedonian God of Battle, son of Ixius, Monarch of the Heavens. Until now, she had shown only superficial deference to the gods encountered upon the Road of Storms. For Mynaeon, however, she ordered the priests to once again raise their altar and burn incense in his honour. She spent near an hour kneeling in silent meditation before joining Guyime and the others at the nearby campfire.

"So," she said when all their tales were told, looking up to scan the faces of this curious band, "you are in thrall to demons."

"I'm not," Lorweth said, frowning a little in pique. "Neither are they," he added, nodding to Seeker and Lexius.

"Neither, in point of fact, are the rest of us," Orsena pointed out. "Strictly speaking. The swords we carry hold the imprisoned essence of demons. We are in communion with them, but they do not command us. In truth, I'm not entirely sure how committed they are to our shared enterprise."

"The Navigator surely is," Shavalla said, chewing a mouthful of hardtack. "Betrayal seems to fuel a demon's hatred more than anything else. Rest assured, this bitch will chase him all the way back to the Infernus to claim the vengeance she craves."

"The Necromancer is driven only by hate," Anselm sighed. "It hates me, and all of you, with a fiery passion. It also longs for the day when this world is populated only by the dead. I think its failure to obstruct us arises from that, for the Desecrator will seek to preserve the living so that they may suffer, something the Necromancer considers an abomination. Also, fulfilling Arkelion's ordained purpose for the Seven Swords would free it from the blade, and the company of our shared companion, who he also hates."

Lyntia lapsed into silence once again, the flames of the campfire dancing in her eyes until she consented to speak again. "I could just take this army and go home. They fear you, it's true, but their loyalty to me outweighs any fear, as I think you know. What will you do then?"

"Proceed to Nahossa without you and attempt to prevent the opening of the Infernus Gate," Guyime said simply.

"And can you? Without an army to clear the way?"

"It's doubtful. But we've faced tall odds before."

"Not so tall as this," Lorweth muttered. By now, Guyime knew the druid well enough to gauge the pitch of his fear, and saw it to be considerable. Yet, come the dawn, he had no doubt Lorweth would still be at his side. The thread that led him through life would allow no other course.

THE ROAD OF STORMS

"When last I trod the Road of Storms," Lyntia said, "I was little more than a girl. Fresh from my ill-advised journey through the Obsidian Cut, grieving the companions lost to my prideful ambition, I walked this road as desolate and wretched a soul as ever lived. In time, a Guhltain warrior found me, a hard woman with grey-streaked hair and many lines and scars to her face. I expected her to kill me, and if she had, I would have welcomed it. Instead, she laughed, got down from her horse and built a fire.

"That night, we shared a meal and she talked for many hours, even though I couldn't understand a single word she said. Strangely, it didn't seem to matter, for I still perceived meaning in her words. This, I knew, was a woman speaking all the secrets she couldn't voice to her own kind. She was unburdening herself. So, when she was done, I did the same. I spoke of the friends I had compelled to follow me on a hopeless quest. Of the guilt I would feel for all my days. Of the brother I hated and the father who roused only pity and despair in my heart. When I finished, she gave me a skin filled with some form of liquor that tasted foul but succeeded in sending me into a very sound sleep. Come the dawn, the Guhltain woman was gone, though she left me water and food enough for the journey to the Pass of Armenion."

Lyntia's features hardened into a resolved frown. "That day I stepped from childhood into womanhood and saw clearly the path ordained for me by these gods that bear witness to our march. My realm is mired in debt, discord, and longing for a glorious past that has become our eternal trap. My brother dreams of conquest and rebuilt empires whilst bargaining for loans that will keep the palace servants paid another year. My father drifts through recurrent crises with only the merest concessions to kingship, haunted by the knowledge that the shades of his forebears regard him with shameful detestation. This must all change, and that is my path. Yet for it to change, Alcedon must survive. And so I am compelled by the evidence of my own eyes to trust the word of this motley collection of strangers."

She stood, obliging them all to do the same. Guyime noted there was an immediacy to their respect now, the enforced formality of before replaced by a genuine regard.

"This I swear in the sight of Mynaeon," Lyntia stated, raising her gaze to the helmed head of the god looming above. "Tomorrow, the Royal Host of Alcedon marches for Nahossa, there to prevent the opening of the Infernus Gate, even though it may cost us every soul who marches to my command, including my own."

Chapter Eight

THE BLOODIED GODDESS

•———(•)———•

L ate the next morning, Anselm returned from patrol bearing the only prisoner to be captured by the Royal Host of Alcedon during this campaign. At first, Guyime thought the fellow beset by some form of illness, given the way he constantly twitched and fidgeted atop the saddle to which he had been bound.

"Found him wandering a mile east of the road, sire," the knight said, grunting as he hauled the fellow down. "There were a few others nearby, all dead. As this one would have been, had we not found him."

Looking the man over, Guyime recognised his garb as that of the northern hill-folk, and would have felt him to possess an impressive stature but for his evident emaciation. His cheekbones were sharp protrusions in a hollowed face, eyes gleaming dull in dark sockets. "Water," he said, the sound issuing from his throat like sand on paper as he took a faltering step towards Guyime. "Please…"

"Not until you talk, dog!" Anselm snapped. The superior disdain in his voice reminded Guyime that, for all his virtues, the young knight remained the product of privilege.

"Here," Guyime said, taking a waterskin from his own saddle and holding it to the captive's mouth. The hill man's throat worked in convulsive heaves as he took in repeated gulps until finally choking to a halt.

"My thanks," he gasped, collapsing to his knees. A measure of reason returned to his eyes as he cast a resigned gaze at the columns marching along the road. "Not a thing to relish, dying thirsty."

"Speak truth and you need not die at all," Guyime said, crouching at the prisoner's side. "You serve the Rebel King, do you not?"

"I did." The man took in a long, shuddering breath. "Though the gods have surely cursed me for it, and they are just in the cursing."

"We found many a murdered soul upon the northern road," Anselm said. "Had you a hand in that?"

"Aye." The admission came in a thin sob, the captive's head slumping. "Though it seems just an old nightmare now. Something done by another hand. For I was mad when I killed. We all were. The witch saw to that."

"The witch bears a dagger, does she not?" Guyime asked him. "And Rajan is under her spell."

The prisoner's head bobbed in confirmation. "Though not all his madness comes from her. Ever since he found that damned tulwar, he has been...changed. That humble but courageous soul who rose against tyranny is gone. Now he thinks only of the next conquest. We were at the gates of Creztina. We had won freedom for the north, but even then I could tell it would never be enough for him. Then the witch appeared at his side one day and his lust for victory became outright madness, one we all shared."

"Yet you appear to have broken the spell," Guyime pressed. "How?"

Guyime hadn't thought this man capable of further shame, yet saw it in the way he closed his eyes and choked down another sob. "It was…the feast," he whispered, tears leaking from his eyes.

"Feast?" Anselm delivered a hard shove of his boot to the prisoner's back. "Speak plainly, man!"

"We… We gathered much by way of supplies on the march north, but it didn't last once we reached the mountains. Upon the Steppes, things got worse. The sick amongst us were the first to drop, then the old ones. Somehow, Rajan and the witch kept us on the road, made us forget our hunger and thirst, at least for a time. When we defeated the Guhltain, we butchered their horses, but the meat didn't last beyond a day or two. No body, no matter how riven with madness, can march without sustenance." The hill man opened his eyes, staring into Guyime's face in search of understanding. "We had none. We had no food. But still, the army needed to march."

He paused, throat working as he tried to force the words out. When they came, it was in a grunting torrent, as if he were trying to expel something poisonous. "The Rebel King ordered a feast. A feast of meat, he promised."

"Meat?" Anselm squinted in puzzlement. "From where?"

The prisoner crouched lower, hands clasped behind his head as he heaved out his confession in a series of pain-filled groans. "The weakest were chosen. Those who wouldn't last another day on the road. An honour, Rajan called it, to succour those who would soon win the greatest victory in all history. He said it was a sacrament. Some knelt willingly and bared their throats to the knife, others fought, but all were slaughtered and taken to the fire pits. It was the smell that broke my madness." He paused, shuddering, scattering dust from the ground as he spoke on, words barely intelligible now. "Not because...it smelt foul. But...because it smelt good. It smelt so good!"

"You utterly vile wretch." Face dark with disgusted anger, Anselm drew a dagger from his belt and dragged the weeping man's head back by his matted hair, baring his throat to the blade. "Sire, I beseech you for leave to administer justice to this creature."

The captive whimpered but made no move to speak nor twist free of Anselm's grip, closing his eyes in acceptance.

"I suspect killing him would be too great a mercy, sir," Guyime said, holding up a hand. "Besides, I believe he still has much to tell us."

Further questioning revealed much of the current state of the Rebel King's horde. The hill man's estimate of their number indicated it had dwindled to under twenty thousand, all infantry since what horses they possessed had gone into the stew pots weeks ago. He described a nightmarish march along the Road of Storms, he and his fellow rebels plodding mile after mile and barely noticing when comrades and kinfolk fell out to perish on the verge. A stark contrast to his advance into southern Alcedon when Rajan had enforced a strict routine of daily ablutions and drill, all long since faded away.

"He barely spoke throughout it all," the prisoner said. "Somewhere along the way, we lost the need for his words. His

The Road of Storms

will alone kept us marching, and fear of the witch. All thought was of the victory he promised, all desire bent only to his ambition. We had become an army of unthinking slaves. But mark you well, when the day of battle comes, they will fight. Of thousands, only I and a few dozen others had the fortitude to break the spell and flee. Now the others have…" He paused to swallow. "…fed, they will be more resolute than ever."

"Do you know what Rajan and the witch expect to find in Nahossa?" Guyime asked. "Why they are so determined to reach the city."

"To conquer, we must have the gods' favour. Or so Rajan claimed, back when he was still making speeches. Only in Nahossa could we obtain it. He never explained how and, in time, we stopped asking."

Straightening from the hill man, Guyime inclined his head at Anselm and they retreated a ways. "Eating their own dead," the knight grated. "I've seen folk reduced to desperate acts, but this…"

"Live long enough and you'll see worse," Guyime assured him. "Our concern is not their crime, but the increased speed of their march. Take your scouts and follow the road until you catch sight of the rebel horde. I must know how far ahead of us they are."

Anselm nodded and settled a baleful glower on the kneeling captive. "And him?"

"Give him a horse, and provisions enough to see him back to the mountains."

"He's a murderer of innocents, not to mention an eater of human flesh. The princess will wish to see justice done. Punishment is required."

"Something else you'll learn as the centuries pass, my youthful friend." Guyime clapped a hand to the knight's pauldron, before turning away to mount his grey mare. "Mercy is not always a kindness. That man has a lifetime of nightmares to look forward to, more than enough to balance the scales."

Once again, Guyime pushed the army as hard as he dared, keeping them on the road well past the fading of the sun. He only called a halt when Lorweth reported seeing a dozen or more soldiers collapse. The god they camped beneath this night was another wholly human figure. According to Lexius, hybrid divinities were confined to the middle and lower ranks of the Alcedonian pantheon. This one was a woman of beauteous form, face and arms raise to the heavens, the stone edifice of her features set in a smile of eternal delight.

"Alphia, shepherdess of the stars," Lyntia named her. "Favourite daughter to Ixius. Whenever my people are about to embark upon a journey, they give homage to Alphia so that she may guide them well."

Guyime offered only a distracted nod by way of reply, his attention fixed upon the road stretching off into the gloom. Anselm had still not returned and, besides the many tracks he read upon the earth, there was little to indicate the distance between this army and their foe.

"She senses a keen anticipation from the Desecrator," Shavalla advised, running a hand over the pommel of the Scarlet Compass. "Also a certain irritation with the Warlord's company, but that's by-the-by." The privateer offered Guyime a regretful grimace. "He's closing upon it, old mate. Unless this army can sprout wings, we have to face it: he's going to get there first."

"We'll rouse the troops well before dawn," Guyime said. "March through the day without rest, if need be. Those who drop out will have to be left behind..."

His words were cut short by a loud growl from Lissah. The caracal twisted in Orsena's arms, climbing up onto the Ultria's shoulders to cast a hiss into the shadowed plain beyond the eastern perimeter. Guyime lacked the cat's nose, but the reason for her distress soon became apparent in the unpleasant scent carried by the wind. A sweet but sickly aroma that mingled sweat with the familiar tang of death.

Yuk! Lakorath spat, the sword thrumming on Guyime's back. *That's a great deal of unwashed humanity, my liege, with nary a thought betwixt them, which is why I didn't sense them before now, in case you wondered.*

"TO ARMS!" Guyime called out before barking orders at the captains to return to their companies. "We are attacked! Form ranks and stand to!"

Lyntia quickly joined her voice to his and soon the army was rushing to assemble itself into the formations drilled into them over weeks on the march.

"I suggest you stay at the head of the line, highness," Guyime advised Lyntia as they both mounted their horses. "Most of your countrymen form the lead companies and will take heart from your presence."

Thankfully, she saw the sense in his words and chose to confine her comment to a question. "And where will you be, General?"

"Everywhere I need to be," he said, before turning to Orsena and Lorweth. "Stay here. I charge you both with care of the princess."

"I should be with you," the Ultria objected. Her fine white steed reared a little as it scented the stink of the rebel horde.

"Without her, we have no army," Guyime said, leaning closer and lowering his voice. "And without an army, we won't reach the gate. Please, Ultria, stay here."

He kicked his heels to the mare's flanks and galloped away before she could answer. Riding the length of the host, he cast orders left and right, kindling discipline and order with reassuring swiftness that said much for the effects of his training. He arranged the companies in two files, one facing east and the other west. When springing a surprise attack at night, it was always preferable to launch assaults from multiple directions to sow as much confusion as possible. He entertained few doubts this was something the Warlord knew full well.

"It occurs to me," he commented to Lakorath as he approached the tail end of the host, "that you haven't yet deigned to enlighten me as to who you believe this demon general might be."

If I'm right, a figure of legend even before my birthing, the demon said. *I'll not speak his true name, but he had many others, the Victor being the one I heard the most. It is in the nature of demon-kind to vie with each other, but for him, war was his sole object. Ancient demonic realms ruled by dynasties older than the span of human time were laid low by his legions, only to be swiftly abandoned thereafter. The Victor had no use for power or spoils. Triumph in battle was his only passion, the more formidable the foe, the better.* The demon paused to chuckle. *And I fancy he's found a worthy opponent in you, my liege.*

THE ROAD OF STORMS

The first attack came when Guyime was still organising the rear-most companies in a protective cordon around the wagon train. The troops at the tail end of the column were all recruits gathered on the road under the command of the hulking Harelion. "Keep your ranks tight," Guyime told him when the telltale clamour of battle erupted from further up the line. "Do not be tempted to break formation regardless of what happens. If we lose these wagons, we lose all."

"I shall, General," Harelion promised, voice fading as Guyime spurred towards the sound of combat. The enemy's point of attack soon became obvious when he saw the glowing red circle of the Morningstar's spinning head lighting the darkness. By the time he reined his mount to a halt alongside the archers, it had stilled to an unmoving orb.

"Merely a test of our line," Seeker called to him. She stood amidst a scattering of bodies, the glow of the enchanted weapon she held slowly fading. Most of the dead had fallen to arrows, bolts, and slingers' pellets, save the dozen or so lying closest to the beast charmer. Guyime picked out the crushed skulls and pulped limbs that told of the Morningstar's work.

"She's not here," Seeker added, nodding to the darkened steppe. "I would know if she was. This is a delay we can't afford, Pilgrim."

"Reaching Nahossa without an army avails us nothing," Guyime returned. Hearing a fresh uproar from the opposite side of the road, he turned his mare about. "Take your archers and reinforce the rearward companies," he told her before spurring away.

The noise arose from the ranks of Shavalla's mercenaries, a discordance of colliding arms and shouts interspersed with the

❖ 101 ❖

screams of the maimed or dying. As he galloped closer, Guyime saw a hundred or more hill-folk charging from the darkness to assault the wall of hired blades. The companies of Alcedonians to either side appeared untouched, though those closest to the scene of battle had begun to shift ranks in order to aid their neighbours.

"Stand where you are!" Guyime barked at their captains. "Eyes front!"

He dragged the mare to a halt at the edge of the mercenaries' line. The ground to their front was littered with rebel bodies, and a far smaller number of armoured sellswords. Their ranks had bowed a little under the pressure, but Shavalla was quick to straighten it.

"Tidy it up, you dogs!" she called out, striding amongst her soldiers to shove them into better order. Catching sight of Guyime, she raised her cutlass in greeting. "They seem awful keen to throw themselves on our steel, old mate. Can't see the sense to it, if I'm honest."

A great uproar of many voices came from the shadows then, loud enough to swallow her words. Guyime had heard the war cries of many a host, but this was not the collective expression of buttressed courage and bravado he knew so well. The animalistic rawness of it bespoke a mingling of deep hunger and fierce hatred, whilst the volume indicated an onrushing force in the thousands.

"They're coming in strength!" he called to Shavalla, urging his mount closer as he gestured to the bodies of the hill-folk. "This was just a preamble." He reached over his shoulder to draw the Nameless Blade, meeting Shavalla's gaze with firm assurance. "I'll summon help. But you have to hold."

THE ROAD OF STORMS

Receiving a grim-faced nod in reply, he trotted the mare to the left of the mercenary company. "Tell Calandra that Lexius must come here," he instructed Lakorath. "Now."

He felt a thrum of reluctance from the sword, for the demon was never fond of communing with the sorceress's soul. Nevertheless, a heartbeat later, he heard a muttered confirmation: *The rat is on his way.*

Guyime rested the blade upon his shoulder and waited. The tumult of the oncoming horde, coupled with their ever more potent stink, caused the mare to stir nervously in a manner that reminded him she was no warhorse. "Steady her," he told Lakorath, feeling the sword thrum once again as the demon exerted his influence over the mare's mind. Her jitters calmed, she barely flinched when the mass of screaming rebels came pelting from the shadows to throw themselves at the mercenary line.

Despite the lack of regimentation, the attackers came on in close-packed order, hammering like a great fist at the armoured ranks of Shavalla's command. Sheer weight of numbers, and unreasoning ferocity, forced the hired blades back several feet at the first rush. Guyime saw many fall beneath the rebels' thrashing blades and limbs. He could hear Shavalla's strident command ringing out above the chaotic song of combat, and glimpsed the red flicker of the Scarlet Compass amidst the crush: "Hold! Hold, you bastards!"

And hold they did. Guyime's mercenary career had taught him that those who fought only for pay could rarely be counted on for overt displays of courage. But, when decently paid, fed, and led, they would always stand their ground. The mixed ranks of veterans and sailors buckled under the pressure of so many determined fighters, but didn't break. At least not yet.

❖ 103 ❖

Seeing yet more rebels rushing from the gloom to add their strength to the effort, he knew it would only be a matter of time. Hundreds had already fallen, but the assault continued with undaunted and insane tenacity.

The Victor was always uncaring of his losses, Lakorath said as Guyime watched another dozen rebels cut down. *And you can't fault his tactics, eh, my liege? He surely knows this bunch of war-whores are your best troops. Wiping them out, regardless of the cost, is greatly to his advantage.*

Given the alarmingly pronounced curve to the mercenary line, Guyime knew that the moment of their doom was not far off. Casting a glance to the right of the bowed ranks, he was relieved to see Lexius reining his stout, piebald pony to a halt, the Kraken's Tooth glowing bright as he raised it above his head in greeting.

"Tell Calandra he is to assault the right flank," he ordered Lakorath, urging the mare forward. "We'll take care of the left."

A stern command to make way parted the ranks of the Alcedonians before him. Once through, Guyime veered towards the mass of rebels. The Nameless Blade scythed down ten at the first sweep, Guyime leaning low to slice the shimmering blue steel through a forest of legs. He angled away to avoid the subsequent flurry of hacking blades and stabbing spears, then turned in again to repeat the process. Even armed with a demon-cursed blade, he could never hack his way through such a multitude, instead opting to inflict sufficient damage to force a diversion from their main objective. Several more bloody harvests achieved the desired result, a hundred or so rebels splitting off to come at him. He cantered back towards the Alcedonian line, killing any rebels who came within reach of the sword, then spurring clear so that the others were swiftly impaled on the spears of the royal host.

As he cantered back towards the rebels, a spear came arcing out of the seething throng to skewer the mare through the neck. Frothing blood, the animal tumbled. Springing free of the saddle, Guyime landed on his feet in time to face a score of charging hill-folk. Gripping the sword in two hands, he whirled, the glowing blade littering the grass with a cascade of bisected torsos and severed heads.

Pausing to survey the main body of rebels, he found them disrupted but still intent on throwing themselves at the sellswords. Their momentum abruptly ceased, however, when a flash of purest light, accompanied by a crack of sundered air, tore a rent through their ranks. The stench of scorched flesh smothered the stink of unwashed bodies, the rebels letting out a collective cry of confused rage, abruptly ended when a second flash wreaked yet more havoc.

Guyime grunted in satisfaction as he watched Lexius unleash bolt after bolt of sorcerous lightning. Although the Nameless Blade couldn't inflict mass destruction, the scholar's wife certainly could. Within moments, what had seemed an irresistible tide of fanatical humanity had become piles of blackened, smoking bodies. When the last cluster had been blasted apart, a quietude settled over the smoke-wreathed scene, broken by the whimpers and occasional cries of mutilated souls nearing death. A few survivors wandered amongst the haze, some even attempting to renew their charge, heedless of hideous burns, only to fall to the mercenaries' steel.

Moving through the mounds of blackened and twisted dead, Guyime cut down several dazed rebels, ignoring

Lakorath's relish as the demon fed upon their blood. *Cooked meats, my liege,* he enthused as the gore seeped into the steel. *What gifts you bring.*

He found Lexius slumped to his knees, his pony vanished, the Kraken's Tooth flickering in his grasp and lines of fatigue etched into his face. Although the sorcerous power he unleashed came from the occupant of the sword, it still exacted a fearsome toll on its bearer. "Too much to hope we're done for the night, I suppose, my lord?" he asked with a wan smile.

Glancing around at the carnage, Guyime was struck by the quiet beyond the moans of those still clinging to life. The stench of roasted flesh concealed any betraying scent, but his well-tuned battle sense told him there were no more enemies nearby.

"Actually, my friend," Guyime said, "I think we may be about to enjoy a lull."

There were more attacks that night, but none to match the scale of the assault on the mercenaries. An hour later, a strong contingent of rebels hurled themselves at the wagon train, swiftly falling to Harelion's vengeful recruits and Seeker's archers. Simultaneously, a far larger group attempted a two-pronged assault against the head of the column, achieving marginally more success. A small detachment of rebels some-how slipped through the main battle line and came close to threatening Princess Lyntia's life. They were swept off their feet by Lorweth's gales and swiftly dispatched by Orsena. Wielding the Conjurer's Blade with all the skill she had learned from Guyime, and aided by her unnatural athleticism, she danced

THE ROAD OF STORMS

through the stunned assassins in a blur, leaving all lifeless on the ground in the space of a heartbeat. This had aroused a grudging expression of thanks from Lyntia, resentful at being denied the chance to display her prowess in personal combat.

"My brother will surely make much of the spectacle of my return to Creztina with an unbloodied sword," she muttered the next morning.

"There's plenty to be had, highness," Guyime pointed out, nodding to the corpses littering the feet of Alphia's statue. A particularly vicious fight had developed beneath the divine monolith during which the Alcedonian infantry displayed a creditable courage and also a marked disinclination towards mercy. Consequently, the goddess's feet had turned a deep shade of red, much to Lyntia's consternation.

"Fetch water!" she commanded a nearby squad of soldiers. "We cannot leave Divine Alphia so besmirched."

"Near five hundred slain," Orsena reported a short while later, having completed her accounting of the army's losses. "With much the same number too injured to march."

"The enemy?" Lyntia asked.

"It's difficult to arrive at a precise number given our scholar's efforts, but I would estimate close to three thousand."

"A decent haul," Guyime mused. "But not enough. The Rebel King still outnumbers us near two to one and has at least a day's march on us." He met Lyntia's gaze. "We cannot tarry here, highness."

"I have wounded in need of tending," she pointed out.

"Leave them. We can allow no further delay." He paused, knowing her likely reaction to what he would say next, but seeing no alternative. "Nor can we spare the troops to guard them."

She stared at him. "Any wounded we leave behind will become prey for the Guhltain."

"Regrettable but unavoidable. You know the stakes of this campaign. We cannot linger. Even this discussion wastes valuable moments better spent on the march."

"I can see why you lost your kingdom. Such carelessness for human life ill befits a monarch."

"As does weakness."

Lyntia's stare turned to fury, her lips twisting as she fought down what Guyime assumed would be an edict stripping him of command. Mastering herself, she took a breath and spoke her orders in a stilted rasp. "Form ranks and make all haste for Nahossa. Three companies will remain to guard the wounded, and I'll hear no more on the matter. Remember, oh Ravager, that you are a king no longer, and but one voice commands this host."

Chapter Nine

THE WOKEN GOD

—)———(·)———(·—

"I'm sorry, sire." Anselm's face was grave as he reined his mount to a halt. He and his cavalry had rejoined the advancing Royal Host at midday, caked in dust from hours of riding the Road of Storms. The knight remained as rigidly hale as always, but his soldiers hunched and swayed in the saddle, dusty faces sagging in exhaustion.

"They've reached the city," Guyime said.

"Half a day back, by my reckoning," Anselm confirmed. "We found plentiful corpses along the road. It seems their… food supply was insufficient to sustain them all. Still, they're present in large numbers."

"You saw nothing else?" Guyime pressed. "Nothing that might indicate powerful sorcery at work?"

"Just the rebel horde standing in a silent cordon around the central precincts. Otherwise, it was quiet." Anselm inclined his head at the handle of the Necromancer's Glaive. "However, this one claims to sense triumph from the Desecrator."

He's not wrong, Lakorath opined. *I can feel it from here. He's mightily pleased about something. To parse the cause, we'll need one more attuned to his moods.*

✣ 109 ✣

"Triumph and discovery, both," Shavalla reported, fingers playing over the flickering blade of the Scarlet Compass. "Albeit tinged with a certain frustration." She grunted a laugh. "Something the Navigator takes great delight in. These demons can be curiously childlike, don't you find?"

Impertinent wench! Lakorath hissed. *I've flayed mortals for less.*

"So, he's found the gate," Guyime concluded. "And yet, if he had opened it, our demons would surely know."

"Finding it is one thing," Lexius said. "But, perhaps, opening it is another."

Mortals and their limited minds, Lakorath scoffed, his thoughts still soured by Shavalla's comment on the nature of demons. *Isn't it obvious why the gate hasn't opened?*

"State your meaning plainly," Guyime told him, drawing the Nameless Blade to regard the flickering glow of the steel.

The Infernus Gate is not some mundane human construction, the demon explained. *It is not fixed to a single spot upon the earth. Its location is a facet of the nature of the realm to which it is linked. The Infernus is infinitely and eternally changeable, and as it changes, so too does the position of the gate. I can sense that it once lay close to here, perhaps for millennia, but has long since moved on.*

"To where?" Guyime demanded.

Wherever the confluence of demonic and human power is strongest, which, frankly, could be anywhere in this malodorous world of yours. It's entirely possible the Desecrator never expected to find it here, merely the knowledge of its current location. Hence his sense of both triumph and frustration.

"Then time is more pressing than ever. And we remain outnumbered." Guyime turned back to Anselm. "I believe it's time I took a closer look at our battlefield."

"It's more accurate to describe Nahossa as a huge temple complex, rather than a city," Lexius explained as they laboured up the steps of a pyramidal base. Atop it sat the tallest statue they had yet encountered. It stood a mile from the outer precincts of the divine city, its subject unusual in that, in place of a perfected human, the vast collection of shaped stone had been formed into a lion.

"Armenion," Lyntia named him. "First amongst the children of Ixius and given dominion over all the beasts of the earth. In time, he came to disdain the human body ordained by his father, preferring the form of a great lion, so that all his subjects would know him their king. The Sunless Steppes were his hunting grounds until they came to be desecrated by the southern migration of the Guhltain."

Guyime felt there to be something regal in the bearing of the huge granite beast, sitting in silent and imperious regard of the sprawl of buildings before it.

"Once there were living quarters for slaves and servants," Lexius continued. "But the histories relate that they were fashioned from wood and set at a remove from the city itself. It appears they've long since vanished."

Surveying the wide avenues and disparate architecture of Nahossa, Guyime saw little similarity to this place and the many cities he had visited in his time. Each temple was different in design. Some consisted of enclosed ground with but one small structure, the sparsely grassed field surrounding them presumably once home to well-kept gardens. Others were monolithic, with tall columns and high sloping walls. A few were austere in the smooth angularity of their construction, whilst some were covered in statues and the roughness that indicated relief carvings. One stood above them all, perhaps the tallest tower Guyime had seen. A featureless marble blade rising to near four hundred feet, topped by a sharp point that shone too bright in the sun to be stone.

"The Celesium," Lexius said. "Crowned in bronze that never tarnishes, so it is claimed. The only monument that could do justice to Ixius, greatest of all gods, whose image is so divine it cannot be captured by human art. A place of great sorcerous power, according to many a legend."

"Which makes it the most likely candidate for the site of the Infernus Gate," Guyime said, his reason borne out by the sight of so many rebels arranged in a circle around the tower's base. More had been stationed in the avenues leading to the city's centre, forming a series of dense cordons through which they would have to fight to reach their goal. He saw a few campsites, a column of black smoke rising from each one. Even at this remove, he caught the smell on the wind and knew what manner of meat would be cooking in those fires.

Had we the leisure to wait, Lakorath chuckled, *we could simply sit and watch them eat themselves out of existence.*

"Not an easy prospect," Lyntia said, casting a shrewd gaze over the defences. "Attack in strength in one place and they'll shift reinforcements to cover it. The avenues are wide, but not so much as to make room for manoeuvre."

THE ROAD OF STORMS

"An assault from multiple directions could work," Anselm suggested. "Lexius can burn a path through one cordon and the druid craft another with his whirlwinds. We force them to divide their strength. I shall most gladly lead my company in charge straight to the Celesium."

"No, you will not," Seeker stated. "I alone shall be the first to Ekiri's side. On this, I will have no argument."

"How do you know she won't simply kill you on sight?" Orsena asked. "We know the Desecrator possesses her in full now, both mind and body."

"You may know it, I do not. Not until I look into my daughter's eyes. And if she strikes me down, then so be it. A just end for one who has failed so badly."

"Just or not," Guyime said, "it's not an end I'm willing to tolerate. We'll stand before her together."

Seeker's face hardened, Guyime sensing a rejection in the unblinking narrowness of her gaze. Whatever transpired, he knew trying to exert any authority over the beast charmer would be pointless.

"Which brings us back to the question of how," Orsena said, gesturing to the city. "I'll not claim any military acumen, but even I can tell that fighting our way in there will cost the lives of every soldier in this army."

"And was that not your object, Ultria?" Lyntia enquired. "Spend the lives of my countrymen so that you could close the gate?"

"Whilst closing the gate is our goal, I would prefer to do so with as little blood spilled as possible. I've seen enough death upon this road."

The assembled captains fell to silence, Guyime feeling their expectation as he continued to track his gaze over the city and the multitude of blighted souls they would soon be forced to destroy. By even his most favourable reckoning, piercing the outer cordon would cost them at least half the army. Next came the equally forbidding prospect of breaking through the solid mass of hill-folk surrounding the Celesium. Even with the aid of the sword bearers, it seemed an impossible task destined to leave this city filled with corpses and the Desecrator free to pursue the Infernus Gate.

Enough death, she says, Lakorath murmured, echoing Orsena. *But you and I know that a plethora of corpses is always the legacy of war. The Warlord found a use for them. Why don't you?*

"Do you sense any change to the Desecrator's mood?" Guyime asked Shavalla. "Anything that would indicate a discovery?"

"Not as yet, old mate," she said. "But the Navigator is keen to point out that he's a clever fellow. If the current whereabouts of the gate can be found here, he'll do so before long."

Guyime raised his gaze to the head of the mighty stone lion above, his brows furrowing. "Ultria," he said, turning to Orsena, "do you think it within the powers of your blade to bring a god to life?"

"I would not ask this of you if our need was not so dire."

Throughout their shared journey, Anselm had never before shown any inclination towards questioning Guyime's judgement or refusing a command. Watching him struggle to contain his evident anger, not to mention repugnance at the task he had been set, Guyime wondered if the young knight was about to forsake his sworn oath to see their mission through to

The Road of Storms

its end. It was some hours before dawn and they stood outside the picket line of Anselm's encamped cavalry. Glancing back at the tethered horses and tents, the knight said, "Come the morrow, I hoped to lead these fine people into the fray, sire. As their captain, forsaking them on the eve of battle is a stain on my honour that may never wash clean."

"You have led them well," Guyime assured him. "But our object here is victory, not glory. We have been granted the chance to save the world entire. Is that not enough?"

He saw Anselm avert his eyes, features twitching in a manner that told Guyime the knight harboured a deeper concern than just a missed chance at martial renown. "My communion with the Necromancer is done via Sir Lorent," Anselm grated with slow deliberation. "He is the barrier that preserves my sanity, my soul, in truth. It is the only way I can tolerate the... feel of it in my mind. To do what you ask would require direct contact with it during a most heinous act."

"For which I am sorry. But long have I known that this mission would take all I can give, even more than just my life. Honour, friendship, the regard of more worthy souls, I'll forsake them all to ensure the Infernus Gate never opens. Such is true of all in this company. Perhaps that is why we were chosen, for I do not believe the cursed blades came to any of us by mere chance. You bear the Necromancer's Glaive for a reason, Sir Anselm. So I must ask that you do this, no matter what it costs you."

The knight closed his eyes, face twitching with both revulsion and acceptance. "I shall do this once," he said. "And only once. Never ask this of me again, sire."

"If fortune smiles and all goes well, I'll never have to."

Dawn broke upon a clouded horizon, casting a reddish haze over the city of Nahossa and raising a small gleam of light from the bronze summit of the Celesium. Standing atop the maned head of Armenion's statue, Guyime saw no change in the ranks of the Rebel King's horde. After his discussion with Anselm, he had spent a tense night organising the Royal Host into the required formation, all the while expecting Shavalla to report a sudden shift in the Desecrator's mood. Yet, as the long hours wore on, she related only a marginal change to his state of frustration.

"His mind is busy," the privateer added. "Searching, discovering. The Navigator senses increasing knowledge, understanding. He hasn't found it yet, but he's close."

"Then let us not allow him the gift of time," Guyime said. "Place your mercenaries directly to the rear of the statue. I trust you'll know when to make your charge."

"One thing, old mate," she said as he started towards Armenion's statue. Turning back, he found her features composed into a previously unseen expression: uncertainty.

"Yes, Captain?" he asked.

She shifted a little in discomfort, clearing her throat before replying with forced joviality. "Just a small request. Got this nagging suspicion that I might just have seen my last dawn." She laughed, shrugging. "Anyways, if it turns out I'm right, I'd like Cora to have this." She touched a hand to the cutlass at her belt. "Keenest blade I ever carried, of mortal fashioning, I mean. I think she'd appreciate it, assuming you could find her."

The Road of Storms

"I will," Guyime assured her. "If I can."

"Right then." After a brief sniff, Shavalla offered him a broad grin and turned smartly about to cast a barrage of orders at her mercenaries. "Off your arses, you dogs! We've work to do!"

Guyime was joined atop the statue by Seeker and Orsena, Lexius and Lorweth having been assigned the role of protecting the princess. Mounted upon her fine black charger, Lyntia would lead the Alcedonian companies, positioned just to the rear of the mercenary vanguard. The entire Royal Host was arrayed at her back in narrow columns five ranks broad by twenty long. Anselm's cavalry and Seeker's archers, still keen to get at the enemy despite the absence of their captains, had already been sent ahead to harass the rebels to the east and west of the main thoroughfare. Given their numbers, Guyime expected they would cause the Warlord little more than irritation, but even that might be useful this day.

"Ready?" he asked Orsena.

Although she had assured him that both she and the Conjurer's Blade were equal to their allotted role this morning, he saw a small, tentative crease in the Ultria's otherwise flawless brow. Noticing his scrutiny, she forced a thin smile. "It's not so much the size of the thing," she said, drawing the curved short sword, "it's the complexity of what lies within it. Centuries of accumulated faith and worship seeped into every facet of every stone. To bring it to life, we must harness it, convert the essence of faith into an animating force. But no two souls ever believed in the same god. Welding such disparate and ancient echoes into a single purpose is…difficult."

"But not impossible?"

Orsena's smile broadened into a brief, sardonic laugh. "I think I stand as living proof that nothing is impossible in this world, your highness."

The doubtful line of her brows shifted into a frown of concentration as she settled her gaze upon the stone beneath their feet, the Conjurer's Blade taking on a deeper glow than Guyime had seen before. Orsena's arms began to shudder as she held tight to the sword. For a being such as her to display any amount of strain bespoke a truly impressive accumulation of demonic power. Previous displays of sorcery from this blade had taken the form of a luminous net enclosing the subject it wished to bring to life. This time, the released energy more resembled a gentle outpouring of pulsing light. It dripped from the Conjurer's Blade to spread across Armenion's broad granite spine, clustering in places to seep into the stone like water absorbed into a sponge.

Hearing a soft exhalation from Orsena, Guyime looked at her face. He saw a similar tension in the set of her features to the moment she had conjured Tempest's wings. However, the prominent muscles of her neck and jaw indicated she was paying a considerably higher price this time. The tremble of her limbs grew more pronounced as the magical glow continued to flow from the sword into the statue, Orsena baring clenched teeth in a sign of mounting agony. At last, the final droplets of light fell from the blade and she let out a convulsive shout, slumping to her knees.

"Ultria?" Guyime crouched at her side, touching her shoulder. "Are you well?"

She ignored the question, pressing a hand to the stone, fingers spread wide and her head cocked as if straining for a

The Road of Storms

distant sound. "It's working," she said, turning to Guyime with a tired smile. "We have ourselves a god, your highness."

"How long until...?" he began, words stumbling to a halt when the great statue beneath their feet shifted its mighty bulk. For a few seconds, the granite rippled like disturbed water, emitting a vast sibilant grinding that soon faded as the essence of the immense monument transformed into flesh. Huge muscles twitched across Armenion's back, fur sprouting in a golden shimmer that spread from the god's nose to its tail, uncoiling from its haunches like a colossal whip. Guyime looked down to see his boots obscured by a thick mane, the myriad golden strands glittering in the burgeoning sun. He staggered as the lion raised his head, Guyime and the others grabbing onto the billowing fur to prevent being tossed away. Then Armenion roared.

Guyime knew this mammoth beast to be the creation of powerful sorcery, but hearing the sound that emerged from its throat, he wondered if Orsena and the Artisan had truly succeeded in crafting a god. The roar smothered all other noise. A bellow of bestial aggression, it swept across the divine city of Nahossa and the waiting host of mindless wretches, full of challenge and dire promise. When it faded and the beast lowered its huge head, Guyime saw a disturbance thrumming the Rebel King's horde. They didn't flee en masse, which would have been too much to hope, but he perceived a new discordance in their ranks that bespoke an army ill at ease.

Not so mindless after all, Lakorath observed. *A vestige of their true selves lingers, enough to make them fear. Yet, still the Warlord's will binds them, even as they stand there and piss themselves in the thousands.* The demon paused to utter an anticipatory sigh. *Such slaughter we'll wreak this day, my liege.*

"Whatever happens, your highness," Orsena said, looking up at him with a grin, "I would like you to know that I do not regret the journey we have shared. For all its many horrors, I have found it far richer in delight."

With that, she lowered her gaze, the Conjurer's Blade flaring bright in her grasp. Armenion, the Lion of the Sunless Steppes, let out another mighty roar and leapt from his plinth to hurl himself at the Rebel Horde.

Chapter Ten

THE BATTLE OF NAHOSSA

<hr/>

Had the rebels forming the outer cordon spanning the main thoroughfare been of sound mind, they would surely have fled before Armenion's charge. Guyime doubted that even the finest, most resolute soldiery in the entire world would have remained in place when confronted by the oncoming sight of a god made flesh. Crouched between the great lion's ears, he saw a wavering of the enemy line just before the first mighty paw descended upon their ranks, but still, not one ran. Their courage, if it could be termed such, availed them nothing. Bodies flew in a brief fountain as Armenion clawed his way through, head dipping to snap his jaws at the plentiful prey, before bounding on.

Looking back, Guyime saw Shavalla leading her mercenaries into the ragged gap in the cordon. Instead of simply following Armenion's bloody path, they fanned out to assault the flanks of the surviving rebels, ensuring the breach remained open. Lyntia was equally quick to lead her host forward, the narrow files of Alcedonian infantry streaming through at the run. In accordance with Guyime's plan, the forward companies wheeled left and right to complete the destruction of the cordon, whilst the main body continued their advance straight towards the Celesium.

The whoosh of a near-missed arrow drew his focus back to the rebels encircling the central tower. As Armenion closed the distance, his breaths sounding like the rhythmic gales of a furious storm, Guyime saw that the tall stone blade of the Celesium rose from a circular raised plaza surrounded by tiered steps. The rebels covered the flat ground around it in a dense mass. He could also see more streaming in from all sides to further thicken their ranks. With his outer perimeter pierced, the Warlord had wisely chosen to strengthen his main line of defence. Seeing how the waiting horde swelled with each passing second, Guyime wondered if even Armenion could claw his way through so many.

More arrows came arcing up from the rebels as Armenion bounded towards them, causing him no more annoyance than a cloud of flies before, snarling, he plunged into their mass. The ferocity of his assault instantly raised another fountain of savaged humanity, denser and bloodier than before. Red rain spattered the fur around Guyime, golden tresses turning crimson as bodies, whole and otherwise, tumbled through the air. Incredibly, one man landed atop Armenion's back unharmed, save for a deep claw mark across his scalp. The injury did nothing to assuage his servitude to the Warlord for, instead of gaping in astonishment at his own survival, he raised his axe and attempted to hack at Orsena's bowed neck. Seeker surged to her feet, the blazing orb of the Morningstar whirling to send the axe wielder flying, his shattered head trailing skull fragments and spilled brains.

THE ROAD OF STORMS

Armenion's course only began to slow when he neared the steps. The hail of arrows, now joined by a barrage of thrown spears, succeeded in provoking an irritated shake of his head, nearly unseating his passengers, before he paused to wreak vengeance upon his tormentors.

"He has to keep going!" Guyime told Orsena. They both held hard to the beast's mane whilst he worried his fanged jaws, drenching them in yet more blood.

"One can't raise a god..." she replied, grimacing as another heave sent them both flailing, "...and expect him to be a slave, your highness. He's a very prideful soul."

Guyime's response died on his lips when Armenion's thrashing came to a sudden, jarring halt. The great beast splayed his legs, Guyime feeling a tense expectation in the twitch of its sinews. Raising himself up to identify the cause of this abrupt stillness, he made out a solitary figure standing at the top of the steps. He was tall, though not especially muscular, his form clad in much the same ragged garb as his army, with no finery to signal his status. Still, the glowing red tulwar he pointed at the ground beneath Armenion's feet made his identity clear. The hue of his blade was a different shade than that of Shavalla's Scarlet Compass, a flickering melange of yellow and red that resembled flame. Guyime felt the air thicken with accumulated sorcery and saw how the surrounding mass of rebels had retreated, creating a broad circle of empty ground between them and the living statue.

Oh dear, Lakorath sighed. *I believe it might be time to forsake your mount, my liege.*

Before Guyime could demand a clarification, a great deafening crack sounded. His first instinct was to duck, suspecting that the Warlord's Tulwar could, like Lexius, summon lightning. Then he realised the sound came from below. Another rose a split second later, accompanied by an ascending curtain of powdered stone and grit. A fresh shudder ran through Armenion, Guyime realising that it arose not from the beast itself, but the ground below.

"What's happening?" he demanded of Lakorath, ducking once again as a blizzard of shattered marble swept up the lion's flanks.

Destruction is the fruit of war, the demon replied. *It stands to reason that it should be the manifestation of the Warlord's power in this realm. Something we probably should have anticipated, in all honesty.*

City walls fell before him, Guyime remembered Evehla's words back in Creztina. *Reports differ as to how this was achieved...*

Armenion roared again, this time in enraged vexation as the shattered marble tiles gave way beneath his feet and his massive form plunged into the cavernous fissure below. He scrabbled at the edges of the hole, trying to arrest his fall, the hiatus allowing Guyime to urge his companions to jump clear. He saw a spasm of maternal anguish pass across Orsena's face as he dragged her upright, but she displayed no further hesitation in following Seeker's example and leaping into the enclosing wall of dust. Guyime lost no time in doing the same, drawing the Nameless Blade in mid-air. He landed close to Seeker, the Morningstar already whirling to smash aside a cluster of charging rebels.

Looking to his right, he saw Orsena performing her deadly dance with the Conjurer's Blade, hill-folk falling around her as she spun. Guyime soon found himself confronted by a dense cohort of rebels a dozen strong, all screaming in frantic challenge as they came at him with spears levelled and axes raised.

Killing them all required the labour of mere seconds, the sword thrumming as Lakorath thrilled at the taste of mortal blood.

I do appreciate a meal seasoned with self-loathing, he mused as the gore seeped into the steel. *Feasting on the flesh of your own kind will do that, I suppose.*

Another roar drew Guyime's gaze to Armenion, the sound this time rich in as much pain as fury. He could only see the god's head, his body now entirely swallowed by the fissure. His jaws snapped continually as a tide of rebels swarmed in from all sides, hacking and stabbing as they plunged into the rent in the ground. A red mist rose as a thousand or more blades tore at the flesh of the giant beast. Orsena had raised the image of a god, but hadn't made him immortal. Armenion thrashed and bucked in his stone snare, killing with every bite, but couldn't free himself. Soon, Guyime saw the god's eyes take on the exhausted cast that told of agony beyond endurance. Within moments, his entire form had been smothered by the frenzied mob of ragged, maddened humanity. The lion's last roar was brief and muted, but Guyime still heard a clear note of prideful defiance until it dwindled to a whimper, then faded to nothing.

Tearing his eyes from the sight, he cast around, finding the pall of raised dust fading fast. He, Orsena, and Seeker stood alone in the midst of the rebel horde. The many bodies of the freshly slain littering the ground conveyed no deterrent to their comrades, for Guyime saw murderous intent writ large on every face.

"Stay together," he said, edging closer to Orsena as she backed towards Seeker. "We need only await the Royal Host…"

"Ekiri," Seeker said, a wild, desperate glint in her eye. Her focus was not on the rebels but the steps ascending to the Celesium plaza.

"Don't!" Guyime warned. "We'll get to her, but we must await the host…"

"No more waiting, Pilgrim." He knew there was no holding the beast charmer then, the need to reach her daughter was too great. After so many miles, and so much searching, asking for patience when Ekiri at last stood only a few hundred yards away was impossible. So, when she sprinted for the steps, the Morningstar describing a flaming spiral as she whirled it, he could only mutter a curse and charge in her wake.

Enemies withered around Seeker as she cut her way through to the steps and began her ascent, smashed, torn and charred by the Morningstar's blazing arcs. Guyime and Orsena followed, moving side by side, glowing blades reaping a deadly harvest from the deranged mob as it attempted to crush them. Not since Saint Maree's Field had Guyime done so much slaughter with the Nameless Blade, and even that grimmest of days seemed merely a child's game next to the havoc he wrought now.

Oh my! Lakorath enthused as the blade absorbed an abundance of bloody nourishment. *This almost makes the last few thousand years seem worthwhile, my liege!*

The combination of three ensorcelled weapons sufficed to carve a bloody path to the steps, wreaking death on a scale that would have sent a sane enemy fleeing. Not so the followers of the Rebel King. Undaunted, they hurled themselves into Guyime's path, clambering over the still-twitching bodies of friend and kin, faces lit with the manic desire to kill. The sheer number of assailants inevitably slowed their progress, the frenzied mass succeeding in separating Orsena and Guyime from Seeker as she continued her unreasoning charge.

THE ROAD OF STORMS

Unwilling to let her face the Warlord alone, Guyime redoubled his efforts, the glow of the Nameless Blade blurring into an azure whirlwind. Yet it wasn't enough. The press of enclosing bodies was too great, forcing him and Orsena to a halt. Fighting back to back, they fended off repeated assaults, creating a wall of dead around them. Amidst the carnage, Guyime darted glances upward, hoping to catch sight of Seeker. His only glimpse was a flicker from the Morningstar's glowing orb, quickly swallowed by the crush.

Soon, the barrier of corpses around Guyime and Orsena became substantial enough to impede their attackers. They clawed and hacked from all sides, just out of reach. The Nameless Blade continued to drink in the blood that covered it, but the hilt and handle were caked in gore, as was Guyime. "I trust, Ultria," he commented to a similarly besmirched Orsena, "you don't find the day's work overly taxing?"

"No more than a light stroll on a summer's eve, your highness," she replied. Despite her flippant cheeriness, the smile he saw beneath the red spatter covering her features betrayed an inner fatigue that had nothing to do with her innate tirelessness of body. She was a being not made for war, after all.

"Good," he grunted, pausing to lop off the arm of a screaming man who launched himself over the top of the piled corpses, a dagger flashing in his grip. "For I fear we are far from done." Reaching out, he pulled her close, her surprise at the gesture overcoming any instinctive resistance. "Forgive me," he said. "And hold tight."

He waited until she had clamped her arms around his chest, then gripped the Nameless Blade in both hands and whirled with all his might. The proximity of so many foes left scant room for this manoeuvre, the sword's tip slicing through limbs and faces before he completed the throwing motion that would cast it into the air. The curse that bound them ensured his grip never faltered, the momentum of the throw and the weapon's demonic energy carrying both him and Orsena aloft. They described an untidy, tumbling arc over the roiling mass of rebels, plummeting down to land hard upon the plaza a few yards from the top-most step.

Surging to his feet, Guyime scanned the plaza for Seeker, at first seeing only hundreds of rebels sprinting across the flat surface, all making for the base of the Celesium. *The Warlord seeks to craft a last line of defence,* Lakorath explained. However, there were still thousands thronging the steps. Those closest to Guyime and Orsena began to surge in pursuit of their prey, then came to an abrupt halt. They stood in frozen, gaped-mouthed silence for the space of a heartbeat, then turned as one to confront a new threat.

Shavalla's mercenaries and Princess Lyntia's personal guard attacked the base of the steps side by side. They had wisely angled their attack to skirt the edge of the chasm housing the corpse of the slain lion god. This ensured the security of their left flank as they thrust into the rebel ranks. The impetus of the charge enabled them to gain the lower steps before resistance stiffened and the advance slowed to a crawl. The weight of rebel numbers might have forced the mercenaries and Alcedonians into the chasm, there to share Armenion's fate, but they were spared by the arrival of the rest of the Royal Host.

The companies came on in a disciplined advance rather than a pell-mell charge, three columns broad. Their long spears took a fearful toll from the rebels as they forced an arcing bow

THE ROAD OF STORMS

in their line. The maddened hill-folk, however, fought back with customary disregard for their lives, bringing the Alcedonians to a halt, whereupon the struggle began to degenerate into a grand, savage melee. Seeing one company overwhelmed by the seething horde, Guyime quelled the impulse to throw himself into the fray. Having trained these soldiers, it pained him to watch so many fall.

It was always part of the plan, my liege, Lakorath reminded him, his arch amusement stirring an unwise, defiant anger in Guyime's breast. He might have followed his instinct and launched himself down the steps if Orsena hadn't reached out to clasp his arm.

"There!" she said, pointing to something through the dozens of rebels running towards the Celesium. Guyime found it quickly: the fiery circle of the Morningstar overlapping with the flaming arc of the Warlord's Tulwar.

Turning his back on the struggle below the plaza, Guyime charged at the glow of ensorcelled weaponry, Orsena close behind. Some maddened hill-folk attempted to bar their path, but were swiftly cut down, whilst most seemed intent on joining the growing cordon around the base of the Celesium. Soon the rebels faded from their path, revealing the sight of the Rebel King engaged in furious battle with Seeker.

They were still a hundred yards off, Guyime accelerating to close the distance as he watched Rajan dodge an overhead swing of the Morningstar. Marble exploded as the glowing ball impacted the plaza before Seeker tore it free and swung again.

"Get you gone from my path, you filth!" she yelled as Rajan's tall form swayed clear of the Morningstar's arc. "I want only my daughter!" Guyime's heart lurched in alarmed fury at the

❖ 129 ❖

sight of the deep, bleeding scar across her face, and others upon her arms and shoulders. She appeared to feel no pain, however, roaring as she whirled once more, yet this time the Rebel King didn't seek to evade the blow, but parry it.

As the flame-red steel of the Warlord's Tulwar met the blazing orb of the Morningstar, a bright flash robbed Guyime of sight. He stumbled and fell, cursing and blinking wet eyes. When the dazzle faded, he got to his feet, then faltered in shock at what lay before him. Seeker lay on her back, the shards of the Morningstar littering the marble paving around her. He could see fragments of the shattered weapon embedded in her chest and neck, still glowing, but with diminishing energy. She moved not at all.

Orsena's challenging cry unfroze him. She lunged for the Rebel King, the Conjurer's Blade aimed at his heart. Rajan sidestepped the thrust with fluid ease, the Warlord's Tulwar slashing out to deliver a riposte with preternatural speed. A mere human form might have found the blow impossible to counter, but not Orsena. Moving with equal swiftness, she raised the Conjurer's Blade in a parry. The two weapons met, emitting the same deafening chime Guyime had last heard at Blackfyre Keep. The sound swept across the plaza, Guyime seeing many of the rebels hurrying to the Celesium stagger to a halt, much as the dire-wights had done in that cursed castle. Their hesitation was brief, however, all resuming their progress whilst the struggle betwixt Ultria and Rebel King continued.

Ducking under a slash of the Conjurer's Blade, Rajan aimed the Warlord's Tulwar at the paving beneath Orsena's feet, the blade flaring bright. Instantly, the marble tiles exploded, Orsena plummeting into the newly created fissure. Seizing his chance, the Rebel King raised the tulwar above his head in preparation for a blow at Orsena's head. Still separated from the scene by a dozen yards, Guyime once again threw the Nameless Blade, the sword's dragging him forward, its point aimed at the Rebel King's chest.

As they closed, Guyime beheld the face of his enemy, seeing a man who must once have been handsome, his grimy features denuded by hunger into something skull-like. He also saw the curious mix of both terror and gratitude in his eyes. Even as the Nameless Blade spitted the Rebel King from chest to spine, Guyime knew him to be a soul fully captured by the demon in his blade. For a brief, rigid moment, they stood entwined. Rajan, once righteous leader of a justified rebellion, coughed blood onto Guyime's face, bared his teeth in a smile of blissful relief.

"Thank...you..." he rasped, the words emerging in a cloud of red. Guyime watched the light fade from his eyes and heard a clang as the Warlord's Tulwar slipped from his grasp. Dragging the Nameless Blade free of Rajan's chest, he let him collapse before rushing to Seeker's side.

Relief blossomed from his lips in a grunt as he pressed a hand to her chest, feeling the small but present swell. The sight of her wounds pained him. The deep cut from her forehead to chin was the worst, but the many shards of metal jutting from her skin made him fear she may be beyond the art of any healer.

Actually, Lakorath interjected, *it's the opposite, my liege. The Morningstar's magic has saved her. The vestiges of it contained in these fragments have seeped into her blood. The power that gave the Black Reaver so many years of life now courses through her veins.*

As if to confirm the demon's judgement, Seeker's eyes snapped open. She dragged in a vast, ragged breath, gaze fixed upon Guyime. "Ekiri!" she demanded.

Looking towards the base of the Celesium, Guyime saw the surrounding cordon of rebels had become a dense wall of unmoving humanity. He had hoped the death of the Rebel King would have robbed these people of the will to resist, but, judging by the undimmed sounds of combat from the direction of the stairs, they fought on with the same pitch of deranged ferocity.

"We've a ways to go yet," he told Seeker. "Can you stand?"

Taking his hand, she levered herself to her feet. Although the wound to her face continued to leak a steady stream of blood, he could feel the vitality in her grip. He also noted how straight she stood as she settled a dark gaze upon the unmoving horde of rebels surrounding the Celesium before her eyes slipped to the fallen tulwar nearby.

"No!" Guyime said, stepping into her path.

"I need it!" she insisted, straining to push him aside. Her strength was considerable, but still he held her off.

"Do you want to become like him?" Guyime stabbed a finger at the limp corpse of the Rebel King. "What kind of mother will Ekiri behold if you do?"

At first, he thought she would fight him. With the very essence of the Morningstar now running in her blood, he worried that the fierce combativeness of the weapon might have made purchase on her soul. Yet, through the red mask covering her face, he saw a glimmer of reluctant understanding. "Then how, Pilgrim?" she asked, desperation rather than defiance in her eyes.

"The Rebel King lies dead," Orsena said. She came to their side, brushing grit from her robe, the result of clambering from the fissure. Nodding to the battle still raging on the steps below, she added, "But still they fight."

The Road of Storms

Surveying the scene, Guyime saw that all order had been lost to the Royal Host. Disciplined companies had dissolved into knots of struggling soldiers amidst a sea of maddened rebels. Repeated flashes of lightning blazed near the centre of the seething mass, Lexius blasting holes in the enemy's ranks, only for them to fill again. Off to the right, whirlwinds cast dozens of hill-folk into the air as Lorweth did his part. Still, the horde of a slain Rebel King fought on.

And so they will, my liege, Lakorath said. *As long as the Warlord's essence lingers in the tulwar.*

Looking at the fallen weapon, Guyime saw the same fire-hued glow upon the blade. It had dimmed but not faded. Through Lakorath, he could feel the spirit roiling within the steel, still exerting its will.

"Can you communicate with him?" he asked Lakorath. "Remind him of Arkelion's purpose. If the Warlord joins with us, he can earn his freedom."

All pointless, I'm afraid. He cares nothing for Arkelion's grand design. That old bastard committed a terrible error in capturing the Warlord. He thought he was enlisting the aid of a peerless general. Instead, he inflicted upon this world a being with an unquenchable lust for victory. There's no reasoning within him, my liege. His rage at your defeat of his vessel is vast. Now he sees you as his ultimate foe, one that must be vanquished regardless of cost.

"Then we destroy it." Guyime stepped closer to the tulwar, bringing the Nameless Blade down hard upon the cursed steel. It spun and clattered in response to the blow, producing the same ear-paining chime. Yet, as it settled, he saw no obvious damage upon its steel.

"She says brute force won't suffice," Orsena said, the Conjurer's Blade flickering in her grasp. "Destroying the essence of a demon requires a great deal more power than we can muster between us."

She right, Lakorath said in grudging agreement. *All five swords might do it, but three are otherwise engaged at present.*

Guyime looked again at the battle raging upon the steps before his eye was drawn to a small glint of green light upon the Road of Storms. Squinting, he saw Anselm riding at the head of a dark mass of running figures. The knight held the Necromancer's Glaive aloft, the blade casting out an emerald glow. The throng at his back was perhaps five thousand strong, but it grew with every yard. As Anselm rode past, the copious dead littering the thoroughfare rose to their feet and followed. Behind the runners came a trail of limpers and crawlers, those so maimed as to lose the power to run, but still commanded by the Necromancer's will. Armenion had reaped a terrible harvest from the Rebel Horde and all were now recalled to battle. As they drew nearer, Guyime could make out a pin-prick scattering of green light amongst the crowd he knew came from their glowing eyes.

By the time the newly raised army of wights struck the rebel horde, it had doubled in size, and grew even larger as hill-folk fell in their droves to the raised dead. Thanks to Anselm's control, aided, Guyime was sure, by Sir Lorent's ever dutiful ghost, the undead horde concentrated their fury on the rebels, skirting the embattled soldiers and mercenaries as they tore through their former comrades. For the first time, Guyime heard shrieks of terror from the enemy. Some were surely finding themselves confronted by the murderous corpse of friend or kin, shock and

THE ROAD OF STORMS

grief combining to undo the Warlord's hold on their minds. He saw dozens fleeing along the Road of Storms, a trickle that swelled to a torrent as the slaughter continued.

Not all were freed from their mental shackles, however. The undead assault succeeded in carving a wide, bloody path to the top of the steps, but many rebels on the flanks kept fighting. Also, when Guyime turned to assess the cordon surrounding the Celesium, he found their ranks as solid as before.

"Call to the Navigator, the Necromancer, and Calandra," Guyime told Lakorath, settling a purposeful gaze upon the Warlord's Tulwar. "It's well past time we finished this."

Chapter Eleven

THE CELESIUM

•)————(•)————(•

By the time the other sword bearers joined them on the plaza, the battle upon the steps was mostly over. When every casualty suffered by an army is instantly transformed into an enemy, defeat is certain. Anselm's legion of wights had spread out across the broad arc of the plaza's edge, killing most and driving many to flee. When Anselm climbed to the top of the steps, Guyime bade him halt his wights, for they needed the full power of his sword. Below, the battle guttered out as Lyntia marshalled the remnants of the Royal Host to cut down the surviving rebels so immersed in the Warlord's snare that no amount of fear could unseat it.

"So," Orsena ventured as the sword bearers gathered around the Warlord's Tulwar, "how is this done? Do we all just hack away at it until it breaks?"

"Nothing so simple," Lexius said. From the troubled crease of his brow as he regarded the flickering blade of the Kraken's Tooth, Guyime divined a palpable dislike of his wife's counsel. "This will be a battle of the spirit. We touch our swords to the tulwar, whereupon the occupants of our blades will do battle with the Warlord."

"Calandra is certain this will work?" Guyime asked. He found the scholar's answering shrug more worrisome than anything he might have uttered. If Lexius couldn't summon words sufficient to the task ahead, then it must be dire indeed.

"We could just forego this, sire," Anselm said. The knight's features were dark with combined pain and repugnance as he nodded to the dense phalanx of rebels surrounding the Celesium. "Those under the Necromancer's sway can carve us a path."

"We don't have time," Shavalla stated. Although uninjured, she was besmirched by combat, the breastplate she wore dented in several places and streaked in gore. In her grasp, the Scarlet Compass pulsed an angry shade of red. "The Desecrator's mind sings a song of discovery. He has what he came for. If we're to prevent him using it, we can't waste time on another battle."

"Enough talk," Guyime said. Stepping forward, he lowered the tip of the Nameless Blade until it almost touched the tulwar's steel. "Are you ready, demon?" he asked Lakorath once the others had followed suit.

My enthusiasm is without bounds, my liege. Guyime sensed the rarely expressed fear beneath the demon's sardonic drawl. But there was also a certain amount of relish that reminded him of this being's essential nature. Demons existed not only to torment mortals but also to dominate their own kind. He would have to ask Lexius to confirm it, but suspected there would be no word in any demon tongue that equated to 'friendship'.

Guyime nodded to the others and, as one, they touched the tips of their swords to the tulwar's blade. He had expected an instantaneous reaction, a shudder at least, so blinked in surprise when the sensation that followed consisted of a

The Road of Storms

curious sense of peace. His mystification as to why was solved by Anselm's gasp.

"They've gone," the knight breathed, a smile appearing on his lips.

"Not quite, young mate," Shavalla said, frowning. "I can still feel her. But it's…different. More distant."

The dim, echoing voice Guyime heard then proved her right. It was undoubtedly Lakorath, but it was as if he called out from the depth of the deepest well. The words were either swallowed by the distance or spoken in a tongue ungraspable by a human mind. Still, he heard the fury in it, and the pain. The only outward manifestation of the struggle came in the mix of glowing colours swirling across the surface of the Warlord's Tulwar.

At first they were chaotic, different shades of red, green, and blue rebounding from each other. Soon, however, the other colours began to coalesce around a deeper shade of crimson, their movement shifting into a vortex. Guyime heard a faint cry of triumph from Lakorath, but it was short-lived when the embattled circle of crimson exploded into smaller swirls, each one battling a different colour. Flecks of each were torn away as the contest continued, the glow of the Warlord's Tulwar flickering so bright Guyime had to shield his eyes. Lakorath was screaming now, the depth of his agony and rage sending a jolt through Guyime's arm. Glancing at his companions, he saw the effects of the struggle reflected in their faces. Lexius was the most distressed, choking back a sob as his sword arm shook. Guyime knew he was fighting the impulse to withdraw the Kraken's Tooth and put an end to his wife's suffering.

Blinking against the thrumming glare, Guyime looked again at the tulwar's blade, seeing how the crimson vortex had grown in size, its smaller parts lashing out like the tentacles of an angry sea beast to tear at the other colours. Lakorath screamed with every blow, the sound now filled with more despair than rage.

The tide of combat shifted when Anselm let out a shout, staggering as the Necromancer's Glaive pulsed with light. This was not the sickly green of the Necromancer, but a flare of pure white. It slipped from the glaive into the tulwar, a small, shining bead that tracked across the ensorcelled steel, the crimson tendrils of the Warlord withering from its path until it met the densest cluster of colour.

"No!" Anselm grunted, Guyime seeing stark desperation in the knight's quivering features. "Please don't!"

The white bead, and Guyime had no doubt which soul it represented, burned its way into the centre of the crimson swirl and exploded with all the fury of a shooting star. The tulwar jerked upon the tiles with released energy, Guyime seeing the Warlord's essence blasted into nothingness. For a moment, all was chaos in the blade as the disparate colours regained their former size. Of the crimson and the white, however, there was no sign.

Guyime shuddered again as the blue of Lakorath's spirit slipped from the tulwar into the Nameless Blade. Guyime expected some sardonic expression of triumph, but the demon remained silent save for a lingering sensation that told of recent suffering.

"Demon?" Guyime asked.

The sword flickered an angry shade of blue. *It turns out killing your own kind is not so easy,* Lakorath said. *I do wonder why mortals are so fond of it.* The sword gave an impatient thrum. *Time is wasting, my liege.*

Casting a gaze around his fellow sword bearers, Guyime saw a mingling of strain and discomfort on each, with Anselm being the most stricken. The knight had collapsed to his knees, his face betraying fear and desperation as he stared at the Necromancer's Glaive. "You can't," he moaned. "You can't leave me alone with him."

"Sir Lorent?" Guyime asked.

Anselm looked up at him with tears leaking from his eyes. "He said he had to. The path of honour left him no other course. Now," the knight grimaced in weary disgust as he clutched the Necromancer's Glaive, "there is just me and him."

"Guyime!" Orsena said, voice urgent with alarm.

Hearing a chorus of screams from the direction of the Celesium, Guyime turned to see the dense cordon of rebels that surrounded it being assailed by Necromancer's wights. The hill-folk appeared incapable of defending themselves, staggering in confusion as the risen dead tore through their ranks.

"Anselm!" Guyime snapped. "Return them to death. We've no need of them now."

"He wants…" Anselm shuddered, his sword pulsing in his grip. "He wants very badly to kill the Desecrator's vessel. His will…" The knight gritted his teeth. "It's so strong. Without Lorent…"

"Fight him!" Guyime commanded, crouching at Anselm's side. "Your will is stronger. I know that. You would not have been chosen to bear that sword if that were not true." He saw sweat beading the knight's brow as he stared into the emerald shimmer of his blade, teeth gritted.

"I can't…" he grated.

"Stand aside, Pilgrim."

Guyime looked up to find Seeker advancing on the kneeling knight, face dark with purpose and dagger in hand. Orsena moved to bar her path, earning a hard backhand blow to the face from the beast charmer, which the Ultria barely seemed to notice.

"Let go!" Seeker yelled, writhing in Orsena's unyielding grasp. "He'll kill her!"

Darting a glance at the slaughter unfolding around the Celesium, Guyime had little doubt she would soon be proven right. Some of the rebels had recovered enough of their wits to fight back, whilst most were still lost in the stupefaction of having been jarred from the Warlord's control. The dark tide of the wights had forged a bloody path to the base of the tower and were only moments away from reaching it.

"Go!" Guyime told Shavalla and Lexius, jerking his head at the Celesium. "Kill as many wights as you can."

Returning his focus to Anselm, he shifted closer, speaking in soft but intent tones. "If the Necromancer kills Ekiri, the Desecrator will find another vessel and all of this will have been for nothing. And even if it succeeds, what will it do then? You've seen its vision for this world, Anselm. It will forge a world of death. Everyone you've ever known will perish and their souls will be forever lost." He paused, hesitant to speak the two names he knew caused this young man so much pain, but there was no option. "Galvin and Elsinora with perish along with all others. Is that what you want? Is the Necromancer feeding on your jealousy? Your hate?"

It was a harsh accusation, but perhaps possessed of enough truth to fire Anselm's anger. Voicing a shout, he gripped the Necromancer's Blade tighter in both gauntleted hands, spitting

THE ROAD OF STORMS

defiance from between gritted teeth. "I am not your slave, demon!"

The glow of the blade flickered and Guyime heard an abrupt change in the ugly song of slaughter from the Celesium. Wights were falling by the dozen, joining the sprawl of those already dispatched by Lexius and Shavalla. When the emerald shimmer of the Necromancer's Glaive finally guttered out, the last of the risen dead collapsed amidst a host of dazed rebels.

"Come on," Guyime said, dragging Anselm to his feet and making for the Celesium at the run. The other sword bearers fell in alongside as they barrelled their way through the loose crowd of hill-folk. Some raised their weapons in fright, but most were too disordered of mind to do more than scurry clear or stand in mute immobility as they were thrust aside. Quickly forcing a passage through to the bare ground beyond the disarrayed cordon, Guyime saw a single door in the base of the tower, lit from within by a yellow glow.

He sprinted for the opening, Seeker and the others close behind. They were barely feet away when a pall of dust and grit exploded from the doorway, driven by a blast of air powerful enough to send them reeling. Guyime felt the sting of jagged stone upon the hand he raised to shield his face before scrambling upright and hurling himself through the opening.

Finding himself in near total darkness, he was forced to pause and extend the Nameless Blade to illuminate the space. The blue light played over a scattering of shattered stone before it fell upon a slender figure standing in the centre of the chamber. Her face was lost to shadow until she raised a slim dagger, the blade of which flared with a bright yellow glow. Guyime had known she would resemble her mother, but the similarity in features was still striking. However, the mocking, almost pitying grin she wore was something he would never have seen on Seeker's lips.

"Too late!" she said, her tone that of a taunting child claiming the last cake. Her grin faltered a little when Seeker came surging from the shadows, rushing towards her with arms outstretched. Guyime saw a stern, accusatory frown on Ekiri's face before she uttered a curt few words: "Not yet, Mother. I still have things to do before I kill you."

The dagger in her grasp flared brighter into a blinding flash and, when it faded, Ekiri was gone and the Celesium echoed with her mother's anguished scream of despair.

Chapter Twelve

THE SHATTERED ARCHIVE

———•———

"I thought it only fitting you should have this." Lyntia regarded the proffered tulwar with a quirked brow until Guyime added, "It's just metal now. All traces of the curse have gone."

Taking the weapon, the princess raised it to catch the rising sun, lips pursed in approval at the perfection of the blade. Below her, what remained of the Royal Host was engaged in digging a series of pits where the copious dead would be laid to rest. Orsena reckoned that little under half had survived the Road of Storms and the subsequent Battle of Nahossa. Given the odds they had faced, Guyime considered this a remarkable achievement, due in no small part to Lyntia's leadership.

The far smaller number of rebel survivors were encamped a quarter mile to the west. There had been some impromptu killings when the Royal Host gained the plaza to find their enemies dazed and defenceless. Anger over the massacres witnessed on the march from Creztina still lingered. Lyntia

❖ 145 ❖

had been quick to put a stop to it, decreeing the rebels had been acting under the influence of vile foreign magics and were therefore subject to amnesty. The rebel contingent remained a bereft, anguished lot. Some were lost to continual weeping and, over the course of the succeeding night, dozens had taken their own lives whilst others simply wandered away into the steppes, crying out in their madness.

"Some might still be able to fight," Guyime said, gesturing to the rebel camp. "You'll need them on the march back. The Guhltain will be keen to avenge this intrusion. Mayhap the Royal Host will have another battle to fight before this is over."

Lyntia lowered the tulwar to regard him with a frown. "Without their general, I assume?"

"Our contract stands complete, highness. And Ultria Orsena assures me all of House Carvaro's obligations will be met in full."

Her lips formed a grim smile as she glanced over her shoulder at the Celesium. "The Infernus Gate. You still need to find it."

"We do. Though where to look is a pressing question."

"Would that I could aid you, but my business lies at home. Besides." She twirled the tulwar, the blade shimmering in the sun. "Without a demon inhabiting this, I doubt I would be of much use."

"And, if I may be so bold, what is your business at home?"

Lyntia turned her gaze to the Road of Storms, letting out a resigned sigh. "Return to Creztina. Wait for my father to die. Kill my brother. And assume the throne. With an army like this at my back, who would dare oppose me?"

"Laudable ambitions. Though if I may offer some parting advice, as your general and one who has seen the rise and fall of many a monarch?"

Arching an eyebrow, she nodded for him to continue.

"You may think it appropriate to wait before killing your brother, but he will not delay in killing you. A snake knows the value of striking first."

"Sage words, as always." Lyntia gave a tight, almost regretful grin and started to descend from the plaza. She paused after a few steps, turning back to him with a mingling of regard and guilt showing in the tensed lines of her face. He heard a small catch in her voice as she spoke on. "Of course, I wish you success. Also, I am not so proud as to pretend that pursuing my own path makes me anything other than a coward. But the road you walk leads only to more of this." She raised her arms, gesturing to the many bodies still littering the steps and the plaza. "And that I cannot face. It is my most fervent hope, if the gods favour me, that my brother's blood will be the last I ever spill. Fare you well, General."

"Not quite right," Lexius mused, finger stroking his chin as he contemplated the shard of marble hovering in the air. "If you could revolve it by a few points to the left, Ultria."

Orsena duly altered the angle of the Conjurer's Blade, flexing the cage of light enmeshing the shard to shift it into a new position. The stone was, in fact, an assemblage of smaller fragments sought out and collected by the Artisan's magic. Orsena's demon possessed a level of insight into form and structure well beyond that of any human mind. In the two days since Princess Lyntia's departure with the Royal Host, Lexius and Orsena had scoured the remnants left by the Desecrator in the instant before Ekiri's disappearance. They had quickly come to the conclusion that the fragments represented an extensive collection of inscribed marble tablets that had covered the walls of this chamber. The pieces they had so far managed to reconstruct were found to be etched with an archaic form of Alcedonian script, as well as various garish depictions of death and mutilation.

"Interesting," Lexius mused, peering closer at the fragment. Guyime knew by now not to hurry the scholar's rumination, but Seeker was not so circumspect.

"Interesting or not," she grated, arms crossed and her scarred features stern with impatience, "does it tell us where she is?"

Lexius was not a soul given to anger, but his magnified eyes did betray a measure of annoyance as he turned to the beast charmer. "This task is complex," he said simply, before resuming his scrutiny.

Seeker's scar puckered as her scowl deepened. The injury had healed quickly, thanks, Guyime assumed, to the lingering effects of having so many pieces of the Morningstar embedded in her flesh. Still, the mark was deep and her face would never recover its smooth and sculpted beauty. This appeared to concern her not at all. For years, her sole focus had been finding her daughter and being denied her prize after coming so close had done much to coarsen an already combative nature.

"We don't have time for your scholarly indulgences…" she began, falling into an annoyed silence when Guyime touched a hand to her shoulder.

"Some air, I think," he said, inclining his head at the doorway.

The Road of Storms

Once outside in the frigid steppe-born winds, Seeker hugged herself, saying nothing, which had become her habit in between bouts of anger. Nearby, Shavalla and Lorweth sat close to a fire, its embers scattering in the breeze, whilst Anselm wandered at the plaza's edge, his gaze roving the plain beyond the city. They lived in constant expectation of the Guhltain's appearance, but as yet, the horse tribes continued to shun the divine city. Lorweth opined that their shamans had advised steering clear of a place so rich in recently unleashed sorcery. If true, Guyime reasoned the steppe folk were wiser than he thought.

"They'll find it," he assured Seeker. "It just takes time."

"Of which we have little," she shot back, then closed her eyes to take a calming breath. When she spoke again, fear had replaced anger. "You heard her. You heard what she said to me."

"I heard what the Desecrator made her say. You saw how it was with the Rebel King. Once freed, he became himself. Ekiri lives, albeit as a prisoner."

"The Rebel King had to die to be free."

"We'll find a way. We always do." It sounded hollow, even to himself, but it was all he could offer her.

Seeker lowered her head, hugging herself tighter. Whatever words she was about to speak were forestalled when Lissah came bounding from the shadows to leap into her arms. As was her wont, the caracal had disappeared on the eve of battle, only to return the next day. Guyime chose not to ponder how well fed she seemed.

He saw Seeker fight tears as the cat rubbed her face across her mistress's chin, all trace of her previous trepidation gone.

Guyime assumed this meant the Morningstar's magic was fading from the beast charmer. It also indicated her miraculous healing was probably done, but he still reckoned it a good thing.

Not quite, my liege, Lakorath reported. *There's still a trace lingering in her veins. She'll probably live well beyond a natural span of mortal years, assuming the world doesn't end in the meantime, that is.*

"Everyone!" Guyime saw Orsena framed in the doorway, beckoning to them all. "It appears we've found something."

"Valkeris." Lexius traced a finger across the script etched into the stone. The Artisan had withdrawn her magic and the fragments now lay on the floor in a loose assemblage. "In point of fact," the scholar continued, "the literal meaning is 'The Place of All Evil and Deceit', which was the long form term for Valkeris in ancient Alcedonian. Their resentment at being conquered never fully faded…"

"Lexius," Guyime cut in.

"Oh. Sorry." The scholar got to his feet, brushing dust from his grey robe. "In summary, I believe these carvings were created to commemorate the disappearance of the Infernus Gate from this tower. The priests who carved them believed that their many sacrifices to the gods had succeeded in achieving this result. Even better, the gods saw fit to visit the gate's presence on their much hated conquerors, moving it to Valkeris. Curiously, if my calculations are correct, the date of this transference coincides with the commencement of the period known as the Great Decline—the gradual disintegration of the Valkerin Empire."

What a load of horse shit, Lakorath sniffed. *More like it simply moved of its own accord and they came up with a rationale later. It does make sense, though, given that the gate is drawn to power. All things considered, it strikes me that the heart of what was once the world's greatest empire might have been the first place we should have looked.*

"Valkeris," Guyime repeated, his memory stirring images of close-packed, odorous tenements where people died as much from hunger and disease as they did from the all-pervasive outlawry that ruled the streets. Some quarters retained a vestige of long-faded glories, but the notion that the portal between this world and the Infernus lay somewhere amidst that endless maze of slum and ruin seemed absurd.

"Where precisely?" he asked Lexius, the scholar replying with an apologetic shake of the head.

"I doubt the priests knew or cared, my lord."

"The Navigator can find it," Shavalla said. "It'll be wherever the Desecrator is, after all."

"Which means he may already be busy opening the bastard thing," Lorweth pointed out with a heavy grimace.

"She thinks not." Shavalla frowned, clasping the handle of the Scarlet Compass. "If he had, the world would already have begun to change. She's certain that he's close, however. Perhaps only hours away from finding it."

"Be awful handy if we could do what he can," Lorweth said. "Moving across a thousand miles in a blink of an eye."

"A card he can play but once a century," Guyime said, recalling Arkelion's words from the Spectral Isle. "He expended thousands of lives getting here, knowing he could transport himself to the gate once he found its location."

"Once a century or not," Seeker grunted. "He's there in Valkeris with Ekiri still in his grasp and the gate within reach, and we are here with no means of reaching him."

"Actually," Orsena said. "I believe I may have an idea about that."